KT-525-993

'There's got to be more to it than you just wanting to stay and help, Trent.'

Even as she spoke, she found it increasingly difficult to control the pounding of her erratic pulse.

'Meaning?' he asked, taking a small step towards her.

'Meaning if you're staying here to...well, because of what's...because of what seems to exist between us at the moment, I don't think that's a valid reason for you staying at all.'

'Why not?' He was almost standing toe-to-toe with her now, and she raised her chin, unable to break the bond flowing between them. 'I don't know what this is, Cely,' he whispered. 'I don't have the faintest idea what exists between us. I only know it's something I've never felt before. It's rare, it's unique, and I won't lie to you. It did factor heavily into my decision to stay and help.'

He placed his hand on her shoulder, his deep words vibrating right through her being. 'I can't seem to get you off my mind. From the moment we met I've been impressed by you. As a doctor, as a mother, as a woman.'

The last three words were said with such heart-felt desire, she began to tremble.

Lucy Clark began writing romance in her early teens, and immediately knew she'd found her 'calling' in life. After working as a secretary in a busy teaching hospital, she turned her hand to writing medical romance. She currently lives in South Australia, with her husband and two children. Lucy largely credits her writing success to the support of her husband, family and friends.

Recent titles by the same author:

THE EMERGENCY DOCTOR'S DAUGHTER*
THE SURGEON'S COURAGEOUS BRIDE
IN HIS SPECIAL CARE
A KNIGHT TO HOLD ON TO

*The A&E

Marden Library
High Street 62/03
Marden TN12 9DP
Tel: 01622 831019

13. MAR 08   Staplehurst Library
(01580 891929)

07 JUN 08

WITHDRAWN 1 JAN 2014

03. JUL 08   26 JAN 2010

01. AUG 08   - 5 MAY 2010

23. OCT 08,   1 8 JUN 2010

1 8 JAN 2012

1 3 JUN 2012

Baynham

Please return on or before the latest date above.
You can renew online at *www.kent.gov.uk/libs*
or by telephone 08458 247 200

CHARTER MARK

CUSTOMER SERVICE EXCELLENCE   **Libraries & Archives**

Kent
County
Council

00884\DTP\RN\07.07   LIB 7

C153283145

THE SURGEON AND THE SINGLE MUM

BY
LUCY CLARK

MILLS & BOON®
Pure reading pleasure

KENT
ARTS & LIBRARIES

C153283145

All the characters in this book have no existence outside
the imagination of the author, and have no relation
whatsoever to anyone bearing the same name or names.
They are not even distantly inspired by any individual
known or unknown to the author, and all the incidents
are pure invention.

All Rights Reserved including the right of reproduction
in whole or in part in any form. This edition is published
by arrangement with Harlequin Enterprises II BV/S.à.r.l.
The text of this publication or any part thereof may
not be reproduced or transmitted in any form or by
any means, electronic or mechanical, including
photocopying, recording, storage in an information
retrieval system, or otherwise, without the written
permission of the publisher.

® and TM are trademarks owned and used by the
trademark owner and/or its licensee. Trademarks marked
with ® are registered with the United Kingdom Patent
Office and/or the Office for Harmonisation in the
Internal Market and in other countries.

First published in Great Britain 2007
Large Print edition 2007
Harlequin Mills & Boon Limited,
Eton House, 18-24 Paradise Road,
Richmond, Surrey TW9 1SR

© Anne Clark and Pete Clark 2007

ISBN: 978 0 263 19378 7

Set in Times Roman 16½ on 20 pt.
17-1207-49879

Printed and bound in Great Britain
by Antony Rowe Ltd, Chippenham, Wiltshire

THE SURGEON AND THE SINGLE MUM

To Janelle, a woman of many talents and gifts.
Thanks for always being there.
2 Cor. 4:18

CHAPTER ONE

'IT CERTAINLY looks dark and stormy outside, Charlie.' Aracely peered out the window into the starless night. She wasn't a big fan of storms and was glad she was toasty and warm, safe inside her home with the fire crackling and the company of her budgie. Her four-and-a-half-year-old son, Robby, was sound asleep and for once she was glad he was the type of boy who slept through anything.

Sitting down in her favourite chair, she picked up the book she'd been reading and flicked to the next page. *The Australian Journal of Surgery* might not be everyone's first choice for light reading but it was certainly Aracely's. At least she was able to read it now without experiencing too many pangs of loss and she marvelled at the difference time made. Five years on since the accident that had dramatically changed the course of her life, Aracely was now content with where she was in life and she'd learned a lot of lessons along the way.

Lightning flooded the sky and she shuddered. 'I hate storms,' she muttered, trying to focus her mind on the journal. When a strange sound came from outside, Aracely sat up straight in her chair. Loud pounding at the front door made her heart jump and a scream escape her lips. Her eyes were wide with fear and apprehension and she was glued to the spot, unable to move.

'Hello?' a male voice called as the pounding came once again. 'Anybody in there? Hello? I need help. I need a phone. I've got injured friends.' The pounding came again and she quickly crossed to the door, wind and rain whipping inside the house the instant she opened it. Her long black curls started flying around her face, obscuring her vision.

'Get in. Quick,' she called. The sooner she could shut the door the better. Pushing her hair back from her face, she slammed the door and stared up at her new visitor. He was tall, bundled

up in warm wet-weather gear and was dripping
wet. He slipped off the hood of his jacket, his
dark brown hair plastered to his head, water
dripping into his deep brown eyes, eyes which
were filled with a mixture of relief and concern.
When he pushed both hands through his hair,
making it stand on end, she felt a small churning
in the pit of her stomach at the unconsciously
sexy gesture. She blinked her eyes, snapping
herself back to the present, realising her
handsome stranger was making a puddle of
water all over her vinyl floor.

'Where's your phone?' He wasn't even
panting, she realised, and if he'd walked up from
the beach, in this weather, it meant he was also
in great physical shape. His eyes scanned the
room and when he spotted the handset on the
table by her chair, he stalked over there. 'I've got
friends out there. We need to get help.'

'In a boat?' She picked up the SES radio and
pointed to the phone. 'That's no good. It's out.'
She pressed the button on the radio and spoke
clearly into it. 'Mags? Are you there?' She
waited and turned to her stranger. 'Are your

friends in a boat? On the beach? What's the deal?' Her mind was racing, working through possible scenarios while she walked to her linen cupboard, pulling out a heap of towels as she waited for Maggie to pick up.

'Greg's on the beach. I managed to drag him to shore with me. Dan and Phil are in the boat. Dan was conscious. I think Phil's hit his head. Can't remember. It all happened too fast.'

Aracely nodded as her sister's voice came through the radio.

'What's up, Cely?'

'I've had a man turn up here—'

'Oh, hallelujah. My prayers have been answered. Is he cute?'

'Maggie!' Aracely was instantly embarrassed and tried not to blush as she tossed the towels at the man, wishing her sister would be serious for just one moment, although she did have to admit, from the looks of him, he was in fact very cute indeed. 'His friends are out in a boat. One's on the beach.'

'Ah.' Maggie's tone changed. 'Billy and I will be right over.'

'Thanks. We'll get organised.' She stalked to the door and put the radio next to her boots so she wouldn't forget it. 'Maggie and Billy will be right over,' she said, as though that explained everything to him.

'What about boat rescue? Police? Emergency services?'

'They've already got their hands full and besides…' She stopped when a fork of lightning filled the sky, to be followed immediately by a loud clap of thunder. 'Billy and Maggie are SES and I'm well trained in rescue techniques.'

'*You* are?' He gave her a slow look as she finished lacing up her sturdy walking boots. 'You're on the rescue team?' he asked, towelling himself down, his hair sticking up even further in short, wet spikes. Aracely thought they made him look even cuter and again she had to ignore the attraction stirring in the pit of her stomach. It was ridiculous that a stranger and one in need of her help could affect her in such a way.

'Hey—don't judge a book by its cover, mate.' She shrugged. 'It's part of life out here, especially in winter when we get storms like tonight.'

She headed out of the room, stopping to check on Robby. He was tangled in the bedcovers and she automatically straightened them around him before pressing a kiss to the top of his head. 'Keep sleeping, my darling,' she whispered, and headed down to her office, returning a moment later with a bundle of keys.

Aracely went to the large cupboard near the door where she kept all her emergency supplies. She could feel the stranger watching her. It wasn't something she was used to—having a man look at her. 'I've lived in this town most of my life and helped out in many a rescue. Besides, living out here on the headland, my place is used as a base for any sea rescue that takes place.' She grinned up at him for a moment. He was still watching her closely. 'See? You couldn't have picked a better house to stumble on.' She put the key into the lock and opened it. 'So what's your name?'

'Trent. Dr Trent Mornington. Can we get going now?'

Aracely dug around in the cupboard, pulling out torches, flares and expertly coiled ropes. 'A doctor, eh? What sort?' She continued, ignoring his impatience.

'Orthopaedic surgeon.'

'Shouldn't you be Mr Mornington, then?' She glanced at him as he tossed the towel over the back of one of her dining-room chairs. Due to the way she'd remodelled her house, her lounge and dining rooms were now one big room.

'I completed my Ph.D. last year. Can we dispense with the formalities? My friends are in danger.'

'So you've said.' Aracely continued at her steady, methodical pace. 'Ph.D., eh? Impressive.'

Trent huffed in exasperation. 'We need to go,' he said, raising his voice slightly. This woman was starting to irritate him in more ways than one. His friends needed help and he needed to give them that help, but for some reason Trent found he couldn't stop watching her. The way she moved, the way she talked, the way she smiled. He had to get out of there, and the sooner the better.

'Keep your voice down, if you don't mind. My son's asleep.'

Trent acknowledged the information with a brief lift of an eyebrow. 'If this storm hasn't woken him up, I sincerely doubt I will.' She had a child? Did that mean she was married? If so, it meant eyes off, Mornington.

'True, but you never know. He's used to the sound of storms. He isn't, however, used to hearing a loud, booming male voice.'

'You're on your own, then?' What was he doing? He didn't need to know whether she was married or not. He wasn't there to find a date, he told himself sternly. In fact, he didn't need to know anything about her other than she had the resources to help him save his friends. He almost willed her to hurry up but as she seemed intent on making chit-chat, despite his objection to it, he thought he may as well play along.

'I'm divorced, if that's what you mean.'

Ah, so she was single. Trent shook his head. He was allowing himself to be distracted once again and that wouldn't do. 'Can we, *please*, get going?'

'Soon. You can't rush these things.' Aracely pulled out a white backpack, which contained her medical supplies, a large green cross on the front.

'Who *are* you?' Trent asked, crossing to her side and bending down to check the contents of the kit.

'Aracely. *Dr* Aracely Smith. M.B.B.S., F.R.A.C.G.P. for Port Wallaby.' She saluted.

'Hmm.' He glanced at her for a moment, then back to the backpack. 'That explains why this is so well stocked.'

'I have consulting rooms and a small operating area at the rear of the house. If you think we'll need saline or other medications that aren't in there, let me know and I'll get them.'

Trent shook his head. 'This looks fine for now. Let's go. Your friends can catch up.' He picked up the backpack and slung it over his shoulder before heading towards the door. Aracely was quick on her feet and grabbed his arm, pulling him back.

'Will you just wait a minute?'

'My friends need help!' He had to keep his focus clear. 'How many times do I need to say it?'

'Obviously a few more. Wow. Are you this quick to operate as well? Look, if we rush out now without the proper back-up, without being full prepared, all we'll be doing is putting ourselves into danger and that'll do your friends no good at all. Safety first at all times. Besides, I can't leave my son alone in the house.' Her tone was firm and commanding and, although he was towering over her, she knew her words carried authority. 'Now, just settle down. We'll get to them as soon as we're ready.'

Trent ground his teeth, his impatience showing, but he also recognised the logic in her words. 'What did you say your name was?'

'Aracely.'

'Does it mean "bossy"?'

She smiled up at him. 'Not that I know of.'

'Well, it should.' He paused and shoved wet hair from his forehead. 'Aracely.' He tested her name and found he liked it.

'Yes?' She took the backpack from him and returned to the cupboard, handing him a coil of rope.

'That's…different.' He shrugged. 'I've never heard it before.' Trent slung the rope over his shoulder and picked up a torch. Aracely straightened and picked up the medical backpack with her right hand. Trent pointed to her left hand, its joints crippled, the fingers curling in, the skin on the back of her hand looking like patchwork due to her numerous skin grafts. 'What happened?'

Aracely followed his gaze. 'Car accident five years ago.'

'Just as well it wasn't your right hand.'

'Why? You know everyone jumps to that conclusion or should I say *right*-handed people jump to that conclusion.'

'You're left-handed?'

'I *was* left handed. I guess I'm now one of the majority as I can't do much with my left hand any more.'

'*Coo-ee.*' The call came from the back of the house. 'Cely?'

'Here,' she called, and a moment later a woman the same height as Aracely came into the room, her short auburn hair bouncing around her face in a mass of wet curls. 'Trent Mornington, my sister, Maggie.'

'Short for Marguerite,' Maggie said as she came into the room. 'Whoo-ee, sis. Why don't handsome men like this come pounding on my door in the middle of a storm?' Maggie held out her hand to Trent.

'Because you're married. Where's Billy?'

'He's loading up the car. You know how he likes to use his own equipment.'

'Does he have stretchers?'

'Yes. He'll meet you at the end of your driveway.'

'Right. Robby's sound asleep but just keep an eye on him. Contact Martin and Keith and get them to meet us on the beach. They would be the closest crew members, right?'

'Right,' Maggie agreed. 'I'll radio through to Kieran as well, let him know what's going on as he's chief of our SES unit.'

'Good. Let me get my coat on and we'll head out.' She turned to Trent. 'I take it you came up the path?'

'Path? What path?'

'You came up through the scrub!' Aracely shook her head, putting her wet-weather gear on, then slung on the backpack, remembering to pick up her SES radio. 'We should put reflectors around the signs leading to the path for just this reason,' she muttered.

'What did I do wrong now?' Trent asked as they headed towards the door.

'Oh, don't mind her,' Maggie said. 'Aracely's a nut about nature and sand-dune stabilisation and stuff like that. The scrub you climbed through can handle it, and it's not as though he's going to be traipsing up and down it on a regular basis,' she finished, redirecting her comments to her sister.

Billy's voice called through on Maggie's radio, saying he was ready for them.

'Finally,' Trent muttered.

'Right. Ready to dash out?' When he nodded, she opened the door and they headed out, Maggie closing the door behind them. They shone their torches as they walked down the drive, making out the headlights of Billy's four-wheel-drive as they drew closer. Trent and Aracely bundled in, Aracely quickly doing introductions as they drove the hundred metres to the top of the path. Billy stopped the car and climbed out, loading himself up with ropes, backpack, lifejackets and two buoys.

'Cely, you take one stretcher,' Billy called, handing it to her. 'Trent, take the other.' The stretchers were made of light aluminium and were folded in two to make them easier to transport in situations like this.

At the top of the path, Aracely called, 'I'll go first. Trent, you follow and, Billy, you're last.'

'Gotcha, Cely,' Billy replied.

'Are you sure there aren't any other people we should get?' Trent called loudly.

'Maggie's calling them. They'll meet us on the beach,' came her reply.

'Hey, by the way,' Billy yelled, 'the creek's flooded. Can't get through to Moonta, or anywhere else for that matter.'

Aracely had thought as much. It would also mean the next few days were going to be hectic, with both minor and major emergencies plus her usual consulting clinics and house calls. How she wished for another doctor in Port Wallaby—just someone who was part time, who could help her out when things like this happened. Of course, it was worse in the winter months, but with the town's increasing population and most of them retirees from Adelaide, Aracely's little rural practice was starting to become unwieldy.

She continued to lead the way along the path

as it zigzagged its way down the steep hill. The beach below, Gates beach, was a small cove with the headland on one side and a large towering cliff on the other. Nice and private in the summer but when storms like this came in, the rocks at the base of the cliff became the biggest danger to anyone unfortunate enough to be out there.

The rain was sleeting in, pelting them hard, making it difficult to see. Just as they reached the sand, Aracely stumbled and was amazed at Trent's quick reflexes as he quickly grabbed her arm, steadying her. 'Thanks,' she said, trying to ignore the way his touch had somehow travelled through the layers of her clothing to make her feel all warm inside. 'Ridiculous,' she muttered.

Shining their torches, they searched the beach. 'Where did you leave your friend?' Aracely asked loudly.

'I pulled him well up onto the sand.' Trent swept the beam of light over the area. 'There. There's Greg.' They all rushed over, Trent and Aracely kneeling by the unconscious man. Billy turned on his spotlight, shining it out onto the ocean in the hope of finding the boat. 'I couldn't risk taking him up the hill in case of further injury, especially as I didn't know there was a path. Greg?' he called to his friend, but there was no response. 'Greg? Can you hear me?'

'Was it a charter fishing boat you were on?' Billy called.

'Yes.'

'Where did you set out from?' Aracely asked.

'This morning? Franklin Harbour.'

'Right. You got blown east by the storm. Engine trouble?'

'Yes.'

Aracely had taken off the medical backpack while they'd been talking and was unzipping it. 'How is he?' she asked, noting Trent had his fingers pressed to Greg's neck.

'Pulse is weaker than before but he's still breathing. You do his obs and I'll bandage his head. It was bleeding earlier.'

'Right,' she called, and pulled out her medical torch before handing the kit over to Trent. He searched through it until he found what he was looking for. He pulled out a pad and ripped open the sterile wrapper before bandaging Greg's head.

'Has he been conscious at all?' she asked, checking Greg's eyes. 'Left one is equal and reacting, right one is sluggish.'

'I haven't been able to rouse him.' Trent finished off the bandage.

'Any breaks?' There was no point hooking on her stethoscope to check his breathing because she wouldn't be able to hear a thing. She was having trouble enough understanding what Trent was saying and they were directly opposite each other and yelling.

'It's too difficult to tell. The bulk of his clothing is inhibiting.'

'We'll need to check him before we move him,' she said.

Trent pulled out a cervical collar and fastened it around Greg's neck. 'Greg. Greg,' Trent yelled, but still received no response.

'I'll check his pulse points,' she said, hoping all of them were working. Her fingers were numb and although she *knew* she was pressing them to Greg's neck, it took a moment and a lot of concentration before she could say whether or not there was a pulse. 'Carotid pulse is weak on both sides,' she reported. Next she checked his radial pulse. It was there on his right but not on his left. She reported this information to Trent.

Quickly, Aracely shifted and firmly wriggled her right hand through Greg's sopping wet clothing in order to get to his brachial pulse at the top of his arm. Finally she found it. 'It's there,' she said. 'He must have a break or a kink in his left arm.' She glanced down at the limb in question but, with the rain still stinging in her eyes and whipping about them, it was difficult to see anything.

'What I wouldn't give for X-ray vision, but as that's never going to happen, I guess we'd better splint his arm before we move him. Trent, can you check his legs?' She then called to her brother-in-law. 'Billy?'

'Yeah?' He came over to her side.

'I need a stick for a splint.'

'Right.'

Trent looked up from his task. 'Any luck with the boat? See anything?'

'It's really difficult. Visibility isn't that good.' Billy went off in search of the stick.

'We've got to find them.' Trent's tone was laced with anxiety and stress and Aracely felt for him.

'Let's just get Greg stabilised,' she said firmly. 'How are his legs?'

Trent shifted around. 'Both posterior tibial pulse on both ankles present,' he reported a moment or two later.

'Excellent.' That at least meant blood was still flowing down Greg's legs. There could still be fractures but, if so, they weren't causing too much damage.

Trent moved to Greg's injured arm, lengthening it slightly in an attempt to get the blood to flow all the way down the arm.

'Any luck?' she called as she once more checked Greg's eyes.

'Yes. I have a radial pulse.'

'Did you want this stick?' Billy called behind Trent, and Trent turned and took the object from him. With wet and cold fingers he pulled another large crêpe bandage from the backpack and began splinting Greg's arm.

'Once you're done, we'll get him onto the stretcher,' Aracely said, knowing Billy had set one up. 'We should give him something in case he wakes up on the trip to the top.'

'Agreed,' Trent said, wiping rain from his face as he finished the bandaging.

'Is he allergic to anything?'

'Not that I'm aware of. Greg's the anaesthetist among us so he's usually the one to know all those things.'

'He knows what you're allergic to?'

'He's a sticky-beak,' Trent yelled, and for the first time since they'd met, Aracely heard humour in his tone.

'I'll give him midazolam.' Aracely administered the dose. It took longer than usual to draw it up but she managed to get her numb fingers working. 'You've known each other long?'

'All of us have been friends since the first day of med school.'

'You're *all* doctors?'

'You sound surprised.'

'And you all managed to get leave at the same time? Good for you.'

'Hey—hey!' Billy called, and they both turned to look. A flare, a bright red flare shot high in the sky. 'It's just to the side of the cliff. The boat's headed for the rocks,' Billy yelled, and now that he had a clear direction in which to shine the light he did, and for a moment all of them paused to stare out into the dark and stormy night where they could just make out a white boat, being tossed about by the swell of the waves getting closer and closer to the rocks at the base of the cliff.

'Aracely, secure Greg.' Trent instructed. 'I hope those other helpers will be here soon.'

'I'll radio them. Get their position.'

'Right.' Trent nodded. 'Billy, let's go.'

'Go?' Aracely looked up at him. He was like a dark giant in the night with the rain all around him. Just then, another bolt of lightning flashed and he looked even more intimidating then before. Aracely stood, not liking the way he towered over her. He was very tall, about six feet five, and as she was five feet seven, there was a big difference. 'You can't just go out there. It isn't safe.'

'They're my friends.' Trent's tone brooked no argument.

'We'll be fine,' Billy agreed, as he helped Trent adjust the lifejacket over his clothes.

'Take good care of Greg, Aracely.' He took one of the lifebuoys Billy had carried down and put it over his shoulder. It appeared there was no talking him out of it and she wondered if he knew just what he was signing up for. Billy was a different story—he'd done this sort of thing before, he was trained for it but, still, with the sea crashing against the rocks… She shook her head. Accidents happened and usually to men who were trying to be heroes.

'Take this.' She handed him the coil of rope he'd dropped earlier. 'I've got enough. Also, use Billy's radio to keep in contact and take the medical backpack. Take it as far as you can. Leave it somewhere safe before you get to the rocks and then once you have the men out, radio us and I can come down and help.' With whatever they found, she added silently. Other sailors and fishermen who'd been caught in storms like this rarely survived. So far, though, both Trent and Greg had managed to come out of it alive and she hoped the odds were equally as good for his other friends.

Trent took the rope Aracely held out to him and for a moment neither of them moved. It was a strange sensation, looking up at the dark shadow of a man she didn't know who could possibly be heading out to his own death. 'Be careful,' she said. 'Both of you.'

Trent nodded then turned and together with Billy headed along the beach, Billy's bright spotlight shining the way. At least they'd be able to sort of see where they were going.

Aracely used her torch and checked Greg over once more, the midazolam having taken effect. His skin was very pale, his lips were blue and there was no doubt that they had to move him, and soon. She radioed to Martin and Keith and discovered they were headed down the path now. When she looked up, she could just see their torches, shining their way towards her. When the two men arrived, she didn't waste any time.

'We're going to need to move him together on the count of three.' Once Greg was secured into the stretcher, the men headed up the path, Aracely radioing Maggie to let her know what was happening. 'I'll come up now, stabilise Greg and then head back down. Trent's going to need help.'

'Copy that.' Her sister's voice crackled through. 'How's Robby?'

'Out for the count.'

Aracely smiled at the words, the warmth of the powerful love she had for her son filling her heart as she headed up the path after checking she hadn't left anything on the beach. 'Good. See you soon. Get the surgery warmed.'

'Already done.'

'Thanks, sis. See you soon.' For a moment she stared back out to where the light shone, the light that indicated Billy and Trent's position. She couldn't see the two men any more, the dark night eating them up and obscuring them from view, but the light was moving, steadily moving forward towards the area where the boat had last been sighted.

'Stay safe,' she whispered, thankful that her brother-in-law knew what he was doing. It was strange. She'd known Trent Mornington for less than an hour yet the thought of anything happening to him made her heart lurch and her stomach twist into knots. She told herself she'd feel the same about anyone risking their lives out there but, still, the feelings wouldn't go away. She wanted Trent to return safe and sound.

CHAPTER TWO

SHE made it to the top of the path just behind the two men.

'Stop for a moment,' she said. 'I need to check him.' She pressed two very cold fingers to Greg's carotid pulse and was pleased she could locate it with ease. 'Right. Let's keep going.'

'Right you are, Doc,' Keith said, and as they headed up towards her house, Aracely took a moment to look back at the dark, storm-lashed beach.

A flash of lightning pierced the sky but it was far too quick and far too bright for her to see anything, although it didn't stop her scanning the area where she thought the men might be. 'One elephant, two elephants, three elephants,' Aracely counted, waiting for the thunder to come. It came, loud and frightening, but it was also eight elephants away from them.

'I won't be long,' she whispered into the night, trying not to imagine exactly what Trent and Billy were doing. She simply prayed they were all right and that they were using their heads to think things through, figuring out the best and safest way to get to the two men still trapped in the boat.

Finally they were at Aracely's house and Maggie opened the door, ushering them in and down to the surgery. 'Robby?' she asked her sister.

'Still sound asleep.'

'Good,' Aracely sighed. That was the worst thing about this type of rescue. She was putting her own life in danger and although she calculated the risks as best she could, sometimes things just happened—as she well knew from personal experience. 'Go right into my examination room,' she told the men and they did as she asked. Aracely shrugged out of her top coat and Maggie immediately took it from her.

'Where are you going to put everyone, Cely?' Maggie asked, once Keith and Martin had helped shift Greg onto the examination bed. Aracely was performing her neurological observations on her first patient before quickly setting up an IV.

'His body temperature is extreme. Maggie, help me cut him out of these clothes—and we'll need blankets. Lots more blankets. As to where I'm going to put everyone? I don't know. I guess if you could move Robby into my bed, that will free up his room. I've got two camp beds and then there's the spare room.'

'The sofa bed,' Maggie said, as they worked in unison to take care of Greg. 'Trent can sleep there.'

'If we get the opportunity to sleep, that is.' Aracely gestured to the window. 'On a night like tonight it's going to feel like it'll last for ever.' They removed the last of Greg's wet clothing and covered him with the heavy cotton blankets that were perfect for warming people up.

'Hold on, Greg. We'll get you sorted out,' she told her still unconscious patient. His lips were still blue, his fingers were totally numb, but she was positive he'd pull through, thanks to Trent. Trent had saved Greg's life and now he was off trying to do the same thing for his other friends. She admired his dedication and desire to help.

Aracely looked out the window again, silently praying Trent was all right.

The rain was sheeting into his face and where he'd adapted to that, he now had sea-spray hitting him as well. Focus. Trent's heart was pounding as he and Billy carefully made their way over the spider-web formation of the rock pools, staying close to the base of the cliff so they didn't get battered by the waves that were rolling in. Both men were focused on what they were doing as there was absolutely no room for error.

'Stop,' Billy yelled, and Trent nodded, glad of a moment to catch his breath. He was unable to believe the pressure in his chest as he sucked in air. On the beach they'd only had to contend with the rain and the wind. Out here the waves were crashing not too far from them, spray soaking them both and threatening to carry them away.

Trent took the spotlight from Billy and slowly moved it over the area they were heading towards. He saw the outline of the boat up ahead and realised they were closer than he'd thought, his mind instantly working through several different scenarios.

'We should use that rock pillar as an anchor.' Trent spoke close to Billy's ear and then pointed out to the large rock, which was not too high and quite thin on top but firm and solid at the base. It was almost midway between where they now stood and the boat.

'Good idea.' Billy sized everything up before taking the coil of rope off his shoulders and tying one end around his body. 'Give me your rope,' he told Trent, and then slung that around his shoulders, putting one arm through the centre. 'You hold the other end of this.' Billy held out the end of the rope, which was tied around him. 'Anchor me,' he yelled, and Trent quickly shifted to put the rope around him in a U-shape. Holding it firmly in both hands, he nodded to Billy who turned and headed out towards the rock.

Trent looked at what they were planning to do. As far as plans went, it was the most solid one they could come up with. The fact that Billy had had the same idea gave him confidence that they could really pull it off. He couldn't think about failing now. Phil and Dan were relying him and he wasn't going to let them down.

Billy was halfway out now but when the next wave crashed in he went over. Trent gripped the rope, anchoring the other man to give stability so Billy could get back to his feet. With his heart pounding wildly, Trent watched as Billy scrambled to his feet, gave a brief wave and then continued out. He let out a relieved breath, reminding himself that Billy had apparently done things like this many times before.

When Billy got to the rock pillar, he tied the second rope around it, then anchored that to himself. Then he took off the first rope and tied that to the pillar as well. 'All right, Trent!'

The yell was loud but was still carried away on the waves. Trent heard, though, and secured the rope around himself, tying it off firmly before making his way out to the rock. Thankfully, he didn't lose his balance, although he nearly went over quite a number of times. 'Give me fifteen hours of surgery any day,' he mumbled to himself.

Finally, he reached the rock and Billy clapped him firmly on the shoulder. 'We'll make a rescue man out of you yet, Doc,' he yelled. Just then the sound of twisted metal and fibreglass crashing against the rocks surrounded them. Both men turned to look as the boat was swept fiercely onto the jagged peaks.

'No!' Trent yelled.

'This is good. This is good,' Billy contradicted him. 'They're closer now. We can get to them. We'll put the lifebuoys around your mates and then we'll haul them in. Ready?' Billy called out, laughing wildly as a wave crashed over them.

'You're insane,' Trent called back.

'You'd better believe it.' Billy's grin was wide.

Was it OK to trust this guy? Aracely had said he was good, had said he'd been in many rescues before, and she wouldn't lie, would she? Not about something like this. Aracely... Trent paused for a second and thought about the woman he'd met that night, the woman who had caused his heart to skip a beat when she'd opened the door, her dark hair whipping about her beautiful elfin face. She'd told him to trust Billy and he would. Goodness knew why he was putting his faith in the words of a woman he'd only just met, but for some reason it seemed right.

Also, it was far too late to go back.

'Ready,' he called, and with the ropes clear of snags and anchored behind them they gingerly moved towards the boat. In the next instant a large wave crashed over them both, sweeping them off their feet, Trent gulping in seawater.

Aracely led the way back to the beach, Keith and Martin following her, carrying the stretcher ready for the next patient. After stabilising Greg, she'd watched as Maggie had picked up Robby and moved him to her bed. Still being in her wet-weather gear, she hadn't wanted to risk waking her son completely by getting him wet, but when Maggie had stopped so she could press a kiss to her son's forehead, love had welled up deep in Aracely's heart and overflowed. With everything she'd been through during the past five years, Robby had been her anchor. He'd been her reason to survive the horrific car accident, her reason to return back to Port Wallaby and her reason for living the life she lived. He was her constant source of delight and everything she did she did for him, to protect him, to raise him in an environment where he was safe and secure as well as loved one hundred per cent.

Even now, as she trudged over the wet sand, fighting back the wind and the rain as they neared the base of the cliff, Robby was at the back of her mind, safe and secure. She shone her torch ahead, wondering how far she should go. She'd walked along this beach, these rock pools almost every day and knew their contours well, but with the elements lashing around her she also knew it would be far too risky to even contemplate heading any further than where the sand met the base of the cliff.

She looked around, calling to Keith and Martin to stop. 'We'll wait here,' she yelled, and both men nodded. There was no point in radioing Billy because if he couldn't answer her it would only bring further consternation to her wild thoughts. What had they found? Were both Billy and Trent safe? Had they been able to get Trent's friends out of the boat? Had they been too late? Was the boat smashed against the rocks?

The wind and rain was biting, especially after the brief respite she'd had up at the house, attending to Greg. She rubbed her wet hands together, trying to keep them from getting too stiff and numb.

'There!' Keith yelled, and all three of them concentrated their beams in one direction. Aracely's heart leapt with delight and was flooded with relief at seeing Billy and Trent heading in their direction, carrying a man between them. They were safe. They were all right. She radioed the news up to Maggie as the men drew closer.

'Aracely? What's wrong with Greg?' Trent's tone was filled with concern.

'Nothing.'

'Then why are you here?'

'To help,' she yelled back, and knelt down to attend to his friend, who'd they'd placed in the waiting stretcher. 'Who's this?'

'Phil.' Trent leant against the closest rock while he caught his breath, and as she pulled the medical torch from the backpack, which had been left against the side of the cliff, Aracely glanced up at him. He was in shadow but due to the light being cast around them from their torches she could see the exhaustion on his face. Adrenaline was starting to wane. He was still wearing his lifejacket and had a rope tied around him in a coil so he didn't trip over it. She was also sure he'd be covered in cuts and bruises.

'I'll go get Dan,' Billy yelled, still full of energy. 'Keith. Come help me,' he instructed, and Keith went willingly, pulling tight on the lifejacket he already wore as part of his SES volunteer uniform.

'Sit down for a minute, Trent,' Aracely suggested as she checked Phil's pupils, but at her words the tiredness seemed to leave Trent and he bent down and pressed his fingers to Phil's carotid pulse.

'He's not good. He's been slipping in and out of consciousness, or at least that's what Dan said. I haven't been able to rouse him. Pulse is weak.'

'We need to move him, and fast.'

'Yes.'

'As soon as Keith gets back, he and Martin can carry Phil up to the house.'

'You go up with them and—'

'Here they are,' Martin cut in. 'That was quick.'

'Dan's not so bad.' Trent stood, picking his way across the rock pools to assist. Martin started getting the second stretcher ready and Aracely breathed a sigh of relief, allowing herself to relax for a brief moment. It was almost over. All of Trent's friends were safe. Trent was safe. He'd done it. Well, with Billy's help, but still Trent had done it. He'd said he'd rescue his friends and he had. Aracely looked over to where he stood, helping his mate, and she realised that a man of Trent Mornington's calibre was rare in this world and she was highly impressed by him.

In the next instant, an enormous wave came up and over them, breaking right where they stood, sweeping all of them off their feet. It came up the beach as well, soaking herself and Phil through and leaving Martin tumbling down before sur-facing and rescuing the second stretcher from being washed out.

Aracely quickly wiped her eyes, blinking out into the darkness of the night, and for a moment her heart lurched into her throat as she couldn't see any of them. Not Keith, not Billy and not

Trent or his friend. She fumbled for her torch, shining it in that direction, and suddenly Trent rose up and in the next instant had yelled something and lunged forward.

It was then Aracely saw that Dan had been picked up in the backwash of the wave and was being dragged out to sea. It all happened so quickly, within the beat of a heart, and in the next instant Trent had grabbed hold of his friend's legs, holding on firmly.

'Trent!' His name, her total concern for him left her lips before she'd even had time to process everything. Another wave looked as though it was about to hit, to pick up Trent and Dan and wash them out once and for all, but Billy was now back up on his feet and was wading through the water to Trent's side to help him.

Aracely's heart was pounding so wildly she almost forgot to breathe. Again she wiped her eyes, trying to see what was happening, and when she saw four men heading in her direction, she shuddered with relief.

This time, when Trent reached her side, he collapsed onto the ground, more than willing to leave Dan in the care of the other men. He was breathing hard and as she shone light around him, she gasped at the trickles of blood being washed down his face.

'You've cut your head,' she stated, and focused the beam.

'I'm fine. How's Phil?'

Aracely looked down at the unconscious man lying in the stretcher. 'Still breathing. Let me look at your head.'

'Later. We need to get moving.' As though he could pull energy reserves from the storm around them, Trent stood and called one of the men over. 'Grab the other end. Aracely, gather up the gear. Let's get to the house.'

Aracely didn't take offence at his words because she could hear the exhaustion in his voice. He was coming to the end of his self-appointed task and the relief he must be feeling at having successfully rescued his friends was taking over.

The men started up the beach and she slung the backpack over her arm and radioed her sister to let her know they were on their way.

'I've got hot soup and coffee prepared,' Maggie radioed back, and Billy gave a whoop of delight.

'That's my wife, gentlemen. My lovely wife has hot soup just waiting for us. Ah, no one cooks as well as my Maggie.'

Aracely was walking just behind Trent and she saw him shake his head. 'Something wrong?'

'Does that guy ever run out of energy?' he asked.

'Billy?' She couldn't help but smile. 'Not that I've noticed, and I've known him for half my life.' When they reached the top of the path, Billy quickly folded down the back seats of his four-wheel-drive and they bundled both patients in.

'We'll walk up to the house,' Keith told her as she and Trent headed around to the front seat.

'We're not going to fit,' Trent said as he opened the door. 'You get in, Aracely. I'll walk up with the men.'

'No. You need to be there for Phil more than I do. I'm used to the walk. It's not that far.'

'Both of you, get in,' Billy ordered briskly. 'Aracely, sit on Trent's lap. As you said, it's not that far. Now!'

Aracely gulped but knew it was pointless to argue with her brother-in-law when he was just trying to do his job. Besides, she told herself, if it was Keith's or Martin's lap she had to sit on, she wouldn't hesitate. They were both friends, both very happily married and it was the most practical thing to do. So why was she so hesitant about sitting on Trent's lap?

He was climbing into the vehicle now, holding out his hand to help her in. She took it, one cold hand into the other, so why did heat rush through her body at such a simple touch? His grip was firm as he helped her in and within another moment she found herself sitting crookedly in his lap.

'Put your arm around my shoulders,' he said, his breath floating around her, and when she shifted to do as she was told, she looked into his eyes, stunned at how close they were. He looked back at her and she felt the butterflies that had seemed to settle in her stomach when she'd first met him that night start to churn with excitement.

When his eyes dipped to her mouth, her lips

parted automatically and she found it difficult to breathe. Back on the beach the wind had whipped around her, the rain had lashed into her and her chest had hurt with the effort of keeping air in her lungs. That feeling was nothing compared to how breathless, how light-headed she felt now.

He swallowed and looked back to her brown eyes, knowing he could drown quite easily in them. This woman, whom he'd met only a few hours ago, had impressed him no end. She was a single mother who had obviously been through a lot in her life, running a medical practice in a small fishing town, and now he could add to that list alluring eyes and a luscious mouth, which appeared to almost be begging him to kiss her.

It was ridiculous. Their emotions were heightened due to what they'd been through since they'd met. That was all there was to it and, besides, he wasn't the type of man to simply follow through on a whim. Whims weren't good. In fact, they were bad and he'd learned that lesson the hard way. What he did admit was that he was aware, *very* aware of Aracely Smith and how his body was presently reacting to hers, but he couldn't be concerned about that now. He had patients to think about.

Billy jerked the car into action and Aracely braced, the moment between herself and Trent broken as she placed her free hand on the dashboard to balance. One of Trent's arms was around her waist, holding her in place, and somehow the warmth of his touch made it through the multiple layers of clothes she wore.

The ride was short, she knew that, so why did it seem to take for ever for Billy to bring the car around to the rear of her house, closer to the clinic's entrance? The instant he stopped the car, she opened the door and clambered out of Trent's embrace, almost glad of the rain. It was cold and wet and was enough to force her mind back to reality.

'Uh…so…where do we take the patients?' Trent asked as he, too, climbed out.

'This way.' She crossed to the clinic doors, which Maggie had opened. 'Put Phil in the second exam room for the moment. We'll need to change our clothes and then we can move him into the operating room. Dan can go in the second bedroom,' she said, and led the way.

She began shedding clothes as she came in, quickly heading into her bedroom to check on Robby and to change into a set of fresh, dry clothes. She was back within a few minutes and found Trent peering into the compact operating room her practice boasted.

He whistled his approval. 'Not bad, Dr Smith.'

'Not bad?' Aracely put her hands on her hips and glared at him, noting the cut on his head had stopped bleeding but would still require cleaning and a sticky plaster before he could even think about treating his friends.

He grinned and the tiredness that had engulfed him earlier seemed to disappear. She caught her breath at the sight and found the same awareness she'd felt when they'd first met flow through her once more. 'You have a good set-up here, Aracely. I'm impressed.'

'Impressed.' She considered the word, then nodded. 'I like that one better. *Much* better.' Why it was important for her to win his approval, his acceptance, she didn't know, but now that she had it, her energy was renewed and she felt as though she could take on the world.

'Where can I change? I presume you have scrubs or something I can wear?'

'I think Maggie's got some clothes you can borrow. I doubt the theatre scrubs I have here will fit you—they're all my size. The gowns, however, are generic.'

'Good to hear.' He took two steps away from her. 'Do observations on Phil while I'm changing. My guess is he'll need a blood transfusion. I don't suppose you have any—'

'I have plasma,' Aracely stated as she followed Trent out of the room.

'Excellent. Maggie,' he called to her sister, and sloshed up the hallway. As he walked away, Aracely noticed him limping slightly and wasn't at all surprised. That last dive he'd performed to rescue Dan from being swept away would have been enough to cause a leg injury, and he'd no doubt been swept off his feet a few times before that as well. Her concern for him grew and although he was showing no outward signs of concussion, she didn't want him keeling over halfway through operating.

Aracely had just finished reviewing Phil when Trent joined her and she gave him the stats. 'Blood pressure is still dropping. I was about to set up the IV line.'

'Good. Do it. He's bleeding somewhere and we're going to have to find where.' He crossed to his friend's side. 'Don't worry, mate. I'm going to take good care of you.' He paused for a moment then helped Aracely get the plasma drip in place. 'Let's move him to the theatre.'

'I'll need to look at your head first.'

'I'm fine,' he stated, and raised a hand to the cut at his hairline.

'You're still bleeding,' she said, and watched as he pulled his fingers away and looked down at the blood there.

He growled and shook his head slightly. 'I thought it had stopped.'

Aracely pulled on a new pair of gloves before crossing to the cupboard and pulling out a small padded bandage and tape. 'Come here. Hold still.' She knew he couldn't argue and was pleased when he did as he was told. 'You're going to have to scooch down a bit. You're far too tall for me to bandage.'

He was standing right in front of her, close to her again. Sea-spray and salt still clung to him, but it was a refreshing scent and one that seemed to suit him. She breathed in his warmth and forced herself to focus, a little surprised to find her fingers trembling as she tried to undo the sterile wrapper on the bandage.

If she didn't look at his eyes, she might be fine. Actually, if she didn't focus on any part of his face other than the bleeding cut at his hairline, she *would* be fine. She dabbed at it with gauze, cleaning the area before quickly applying the bandage and tape, working fast so she could step away from him and get some perspective on the situation sooner rather than later.

He was just another doctor, a temporary colleague who would no doubt be gone from her life in less than twenty-four hours. That's all he was. No more, no less. So this ridiculous attraction she felt towards him was nothing more than a passing fancy and one that would definitely pass once he left and she never saw him again.

'Finished,' she said, her tone a little over-bright as she took two steps back, almost crashing into the free-standing lamp.

'Appreciated.' Trent's tone was a little deeper than usual and the vibrations from his voice made her glance at him when she really shouldn't have. Their eyes held for a long moment and it was as though they were both acknowledging that something strange was going on between them but that neither of them was willing to do anything about it. Different places. They came from different places. She lived in Port Wallaby and he lived half the country away in Sydney. He would be gone soon and she would stay here for the rest of her life and raise her son in a secure and happy rural environment…an environment that didn't include the dashing orthopaedic surgeon before her.

CHAPTER THREE

'CELY.'

She jerked her head around to look at her brother-in-law, who'd suddenly appeared in the doorway. 'Billy?' She cleared her throat and walked carefully around Trent. 'Something wrong?'

'I'm heading off. Just got a call from Kieran to say I'm needed elsewhere.'

'OK.' She kissed his cheek. 'Thanks so much for your help and you stay safe.'

'You betcha!' Billy quickly held his hand out to Trent. 'Brilliant job out there, mate,' he enthused. 'This guy, Cely, knows how to tie ropes, kept a cool, clear head and was almost as crazy as I was. You could easily get a job in rescue, Trent.'

'I'll pass,' Trent said with a smile, then checked Phil's observations again, the smile fading. 'Aracely, we need to get him into the operating room now.'

'Of course.'

'I'll leave you to do the clean-up,' Billy said, and headed off.

Aracely turned back to Trent and for the first time since he'd entered the room she took stock of what he was wearing. He was dressed in a warm black turtle-neck jumper, which she couldn't recall ever seeing on her brother-in-law, a pair of denim jeans which, although riding low on his hips, still came to the top of his ankles, and his feet were encased in a pair of thick socks. Aracely's gaze was stuck on the jeans he wore and her lips twitched at the sight.

'Don't say a word,' he warned.

'About what? How your ankles might get cold?'

'Hey—the clothes are clean and dry. I'm not going to look a gift horse in the mouth by refusing them.'

'True. They just look so…cute…and…short.'

'Fine. You've had your fun. We need to get ready.'

'For?' She'd made the mistake of looking at

him, of meeting his eyes while she'd been teasing him, and, seeing the humour light his face, she'd become mesmerised. He was a very handsome man.

'Operating on Phil.'

It was then Aracely snapped out of it and looked at their patient. 'Of course.'

'Let's get him moved.'

Maggie came and helped them before returning to look after Greg and Dan.

'Does Maggie have any training? I mean, is she a nurse?' They were removing the last of Phil's wet clothing and covering him with warm blankets.

'Just first aid trained but she's used to helping out in these types of emergencies.'

'And your son? Still sleeping soundly?'

'He was when I checked on him a short while ago.'

Trent had walked around to the other side of the operating table and was winding the blood-pressure cuff around Phil's arm. 'Phil hit his head badly on the boat and passed out. Dan had managed to tie Phil to the boat to stop him from being washed overboard and when we found him the ropes were pretty tight around his abdomen, as you can see from the rope burns.'

Aracely checked Phil's pupils and found them still sluggish.

'His BP's still dropping. He's bleeding somewhere.'

'Internal bleed?'

'Yes.' Trent turned and headed to the sink, washing his hands. 'Have you administered an anaesthetic before?'

'Yes. I've trained in anaesthetics.'

'Excellent. I think midazolam again to start off with. You can top it up later if needed.'

'Agreed.' She paused for a moment. 'I think I should warn you, Trent, that I'm not that good in Theatre. I can operate on minor things, stitch people up, give anaesthetics, that sort of thing, but you must have seen how I had difficulty even using the scissors to cut off Phil's clothes.'

'But you got there in the end.'

'Exactly but, just so you know, operating with me assisting you will be slow. For all intents and purposes, I only have the use of one hand.'

Trent nodded. 'We'll manage. Administer the midazolam and then get scrubbed.'

'What are you expecting to find?' she asked as she pulled out the items she needed. She could use her left hand as an anchor and was able to hold things, such as the vial containing the midazolam, while she drew the injection with her right hand.

'Seromuscular rupture, just for starters,' he said absently, and when Aracely raised her eyes to his, she found him watching her. 'You're doing quite well,' he commented, pointing to her hand.

Aracely shrugged. 'It's amazing the way the brain adapts after an injury.'

'Were you driving the car?'

'I was in a taxi.'

'Oh. In Adelaide?'

'No. Sydney.'

'Really? And you said this was five years ago?'

'Why so interested?'

'I might have treated you, especially if you were taken to Sydney General.'

'I was, but you didn't treat me.'

'How do you know?'

She raised her eyebrows. 'Because I was the patient. Doctors in A and E don't necessarily remember every patient they see but the patients, who only see a handful of doctors, remember who they are.'

'True. So who treated you?'

'Arnold Prescott.'

Trent raised his eyebrows as he finished scrubbing and elbowed open the cupboard marked STERILE TOWELS. 'The big cheese?'

Aracely smiled as she administered the midazolam through Phil's saline drip. She checked the plasma bag and was pleased to see them both working. Hopefully, the extra fluids should help replace whatever blood he'd lost, and his BP would soon stabilise or at least buy Trent some more time until he could find the bleeder.

'So you were treated by Prescott? Head of Orthopaedics and my old boss, now my colleague.'

'Yes.'

'Why? I mean, he usually only treats the rich and famous.'

'And staff members as well.'

'You were on staff at Sydney General?'

'For six months.'

'Before your accident?'

'Yes.' Aracely couldn't look at him. It had been the worst six months of her life and she almost hadn't survived them.

'You said five years ago?'

'Yes.'

'And your son is how old?'

'Robby's four and a half.'

'You were pregnant with him?'

'Just finished the first trimester.' Aracely glanced up and met his eyes. 'I thought I'd lost him but he's a tough little cookie, my Robby.'

'And your…' Trent stopped and cleared his throat and she wasn't sure whether it was on purpose or just coincidence. 'Husband? Was he in the taxi, too?'

'No.'

There was an uncomfortable pause between them yet she wasn't exactly sure why. Perhaps it had something to do with the magnetic frisson which existed between them and seemed to be increasing the more time they spent together. She found it impossible to believe that Trent was actually interested in her yet from what had happened between them so far, it appeared the impossible might actually *be* possible. No. She couldn't think like that. He wasn't going to be there for long, she kept telling herself, looking away and breaking the bond he appeared to hold over her.

'Uh…' Aracely couldn't believe how nervous her voice sounded. 'You were working in Sydney at that time?'

'Yes, although I did take some time off. A few months.' He shrugged and looked away. 'Personal time.'

Aracely picked up on an undercurrent but decided if Trent wanted to tell her the intimate details of his life, that was his choice. She wasn't about to push him. 'Things weren't going well for you either?'

'You could say that.' His words were soft but he took a breath and said more clearly, 'So you used to live and work in Sydney?'

'Yes. When my marriage broke up, I moved back home.'

'I take it Port Wallaby's home?'

'That's right.'

'You wouldn't think of leaving again? Heading back to the city?'

'No. I'm set up here now and it's the best place for Robby to be.'

'So far away from his father?'

Aracely frowned, surprised at the gruffness that had crept into Trent's tone. She wasn't sure why but she got the feeling Trent was judging her in some way. Did he think she'd taken Robby away from his father? 'Robby's father wants nothing to do with him,' she stated firmly. 'So it's just me and my son.'

'And your sister and her husband.'

'My parents also live around here but they're travelling at present.'

'A loving family.' He nodded though she could see a flicker of sadness in his eyes. She wanted to ask him some questions, to find out whether he had any family. A wife? Children of his own? But the instant she'd opened her mouth she saw a mask come over his face and she could see that he was shutting her out. It was odd that she should be able to read him so easily so soon after meeting him but she was already coming to realise that what was between them was far from ordinary. It was as though they knew each other—somehow—and she was at a loss to explain it any more logically than that.

She checked Phil's vitals again, Trent having found the instruments he'd needed while she'd carefully scrubbed her hands and pulled on a gown.

'You're extremely well stocked. I'm now *considerably* impressed.'

'A step up in the world. I'm very well supported here, on the Yorke Peninsula. There's a hospital in Moonta, one in Wallaroo. Maitland has a hospital and all of them have specialists who come from Adelaide to consult here. All of them have operating rooms, hospital beds and staff who are competent and trained to perfection.'

'And here in Port Wallaby, there's a GP who's obviously overworked.'

'How did you draw that conclusion?'

'Am I wrong?'

'No.'

'Your set-up is evidence that you have a thriving practice. You have two consulting rooms, which may mean you're either looking for another GP to come and lighten the load or else you have someone come and consult here on an irregular basis.'

'The first one. I'd love to get another GP in here but my patients are usually pretty good and Moonta isn't that far from where we are. It just seems that in the last few years my workload has doubled.'

'Don't have time to stop for lunch?'

'Exactly, although Maggie forces me to every day and it's hard to ignore my sister's cooking. Also, it gives me time to spend with Robby.'

'When does he start school?'

'Next year. It'll be strange not having him around as much during the day.' As they chatted, they were both working on Phil. Trent had slathered antiseptic on his friend's abdomen and draped it. Aracely shifted the light using her wrists and as he got ready to make his incision, she was ready with the gauze to swab the area.

'I'll be specific,' he told her. 'That's usually the easiest way when I'm operating with new people.'

'And especially with a doctor who only has the use of one hand.' Aracely was all set up to monitor Phil's blood pressure, the cuff around his arm, which she could check at regular intervals.

'Have you done much surgical work before?'

'Before my accident? Yes. Two years regis-trar.' Aracely nodded.

'Oh.' That surprised him and Trent knew he shouldn't have judged a book by its cover. When he'd first met Aracely Smith, he'd simply thought she was someone who could lend him her phone so he could call for help. Then she'd not only provided the help but had turned out to be a GP with a thoughtful and competent medical set-up. A single mother, living and thriving in her home town, and now she was revealing she'd done surgery! He glanced at her hand, the fingers all curled and contained within the theatre glove.

Aracely followed his eyes. 'The first doctor who saw the state of my hand wanted to amputate. Dr Prescott decided otherwise.'

'Sounds like Prescott.' Trent nodded. 'What speciality did you do?'

'Plastics.' She checked Phil's blood pressure and reported it was the same as before.

'Fantastic. Can you hold this retractor,

please?' She did as she was asked and watched as he packed the wound with gauze to soak up the excess blood, glad that what he was seeing was darker red blood rather than bright red arterial blood. 'This is looking good. He may have clotted.'

'Hold the retractor. I'll take his blood pressure.' It was an interesting way to operate, Trent thought as he removed some more gauze with his other hand and then angled the operating light to shine as much light into the wound as he could.

His eyes widened. 'Fresh blood.'

'BP's dropping,' she said, and quickly lowered the air on the cuff before grabbing the retractor again.

'Where is it?' Trent started searching, looking quickly for the offending artery. He packed the area with gauze and let it soak up what it could. Taking it out, he took another look. 'There. Got it.' He reached for the locking scissors and clamped it off. 'I'm going to do a quick check to make sure there's nothing else happening then I'll suture it off.' As Trent did the exploratory, he noted the bladder had ruptured.

'Phil had probably voided due to the pelvic injury but—' Aracely began.

'It would have been impossible to tell with all the seawater and rain and drenched clothes,' Trent finished. 'Let's get this repaired.'

Again, it was slow going and Trent forced himself to be patient and finally they were able to close Phil up. 'Let's get that X-ray and see what sort of damage Phil's done to his pelvis. I don't suppose you have traction ropes?' Trent pulled his gloves off and tossed them into the bin.

'No, sorry. Moonta hospital has Hamilton-Russell traction. I'm set up for emergencies and clinics here. However, as we can't get Phil to Moonta until the storm passes, I'm sure we could fashion something if necessary.'

'Improvisation medicine?' Trent removed his mask and raised his eyebrows, smiling at her. The action caused that now familiar stirring in the pit of her stomach.

'Welcome to the world of general practice.' She couldn't help the small twitch of her lips and Trent nodded enjoying the way her eyes seemed to light up. Even with her theatre gown on, her hair back behind a cap, the mask pulled down beneath her chin, she radiated a beauty he'd rarely seen. It came from within and even though he knew her to be tired, she appeared refreshed and ready to tackle the next challenge life threw at her.

As Aracely set up the digital X-ray machine, Trent took Phil's vitals and was pleased with the readings. 'Good. This is good.'

'Help me to position this, please.' she said.

Trent whistled when he saw her machine. 'OK. Now I'm beyond impressed. Your newest piece of equipment?'

'My pride and joy—well, as far as medical equipment goes.'

His eyes twinkled at her words. 'Must have cost a tidy sum.'

'Government grant,' she said with a shrug. 'I've become very good at filling in applications and being awarded the money. That's how I managed to remodel my home.'

'How long ago did you do all this?'

'Four years ago, just after I finished most of my rehab. I needed to be able to work from home not only because of my physical limitations—I had bad scarring on my leg but thanks to physio and the course of time, the muscles have repaired themselves—but mainly because of Robby.'

'You don't let anything hold you back from getting what you want,' he stated.

'I guess. I've never really thought about it. I just do what I have to do.'

Trent nodded and helped her move the machine into the position he needed. They walked over to the doorway, Aracely holding the remote control in her hand. They stood there, side by side. He was close, so close he had to put his arm behind her and turn side on so they both fitted into the small space. His chest pressed against her shoulder and she was so acutely aware of him that her fingers start to tremble.

Even after she'd pressed the button, neither of them moved. Aracely slowly raised her head and looked up at Trent. He was looking down at her as though he'd just made an amazing new discovery but had no idea what to do about it.

'Aracely?' His tone was soft.

'Mmm?'

'Was it the car accident that stopped you from doing surgery?'

It was the last thing she'd expected him to say, although she wasn't sure why. He was a doctor and it was an occupational hazard to diagnose or speculate on a person's injuries and symptoms. She, herself, was guilty of that as well, but from where she'd been standing, he'd been looking down at her as a man who held an awareness of her as a woman, and she'd expected him to say something completely different.

'Yes.' She forced herself to move away, crossing to the machine and pressing the buttons to bring up the image. 'Come take a look,' she said, and he came to stand beside her once again. She was becoming more and more aware of him. It would pass, she told herself. He would be out of there by tomorrow afternoon at the latest and then she'd be able to get back on with her life and forget ever having met Trent Mornington.

'Why?' he asked.

'Why what?'

'Why did you let the accident stop you from pursuing surgery?'

Aracely looked at him as though he'd just grown another head. 'My hand,' she stated, and held it up for him to see.

'I can see that.' He shrugged. 'I'm just surprised it stopped you, that's all.'

'What's that supposed to mean?'

'Nothing. Look, I didn't mean to offend you. I'm sorry. Forget I ever said anything.'

Aracely could see his contrition was genuine and decided to drop the subject. Besides, she'd worked long and hard over the years to get where she was and although she had always dreamed of becoming a surgeon, she'd also known that giving up those dreams had been for the best.

Trent studied the view on the X-ray machine. 'Just as I thought. Pelvis is fractured in two places and the breaks look quite clean.'

'Did you want another angle?'

'No. This is fine for now. Once we get him back to Sydney, he'll need three-dimensional scans and images, but I usually like to let pelvic fractures sit for at least seven to ten days before operating. There's plenty of time.'

'Let me guess. You're the pelvic fracture expert.'

Trent smiled. 'My sub-speciality is lower limb so I've seen a few fractured pelvises in my time.

'Fair enough.' She nodded, then looked down at his own leg. 'So what's the verdict on that?' She pointed.

He shrugged. 'Muscle damage. It's nothing.'

'Sure. Right. Nothing. Don't believe you. You're also probably littered with scratches and bruises all over your body. Believe me. I've seen what some of the rescuers look like once they've finished.'

Trent shrugged. 'I don't have time to deal with my problems now. There are other matters I need to attend to.'

'Such as?' Aracely waited a moment for him to speak but he only turned and took off his gown and cap. 'Wow. That's a long list,' she teased, when he didn't say anything. 'You're a surgeon, Trent. Sit down and let me take a look at your leg. You need to rest because if it *is* muscular, you risk doing further damage the longer you stay on it.'

'I need to check on Greg and Dan. Take care of Phil for me.'

'I'll do that, and once you're finished I'll

expect you to come and help me move Phil. When all your patients are satisfactorily settled, I'll be taking a look at your leg, Dr Mornington, and that's all there is to it.'

Trent turned and headed to the doorway, content to leave Phil in Aracely's care, but he paused and looked at her over his shoulder. 'Are you *sure* your name doesn't mean "bossy"?'

CHAPTER FOUR

'HERE.' Maggie came into the room where Aracely was looking after Greg. 'Drink this. It's nice sugary tea. You need it.'

Aracely and Trent had just finished applying a cast to Greg's arm and Trent was now checking on Dan. Phil was recovering well, his BP increasing, and Trent was pleased with his friend's progress.

'Green?' Maggie asked, pointing to colour of Greg's cast.

Aracely shrugged. 'Thought he might like it. How are you holding up, sis?'

'Fair.' Maggie sat on the chair in the corner. 'Billy's just radioed in to say the storm's playing havoc with everyone and everything. He called it a humdinger of a storm.'

Aracely watched as Maggie rubbed a hand

over her still flat stomach. 'Are you sure you're feeling all right?'

'Fine. Indigestion, I guess.'

'Well, you remember to rest and keep off your feet. Sit down as much as possible. I'll not have anything happening to Robby's cousin.'

'*Robby* won't let anything happen to his cousin. Your son has a definite protective streak.'

'Good to hear. Young boys need to understand the importance of family in this day and age,' Trent said as he came into the room. He was still limping but Aracely could tell he was also trying to play it down. She gave him a look that said he didn't fool her for a moment, to which he merely shrugged before checking Greg's temperature. 'Now you're getting there, old friend. Temperature's almost normal.'

'He is recovering well,' Aracely agreed.

Trent then fixed his eyes on Maggie. 'Sorry to pry but I couldn't help overhearing. You're pregnant?'

'Yes.' Maggie's smile was full faced and Aracely loved seeing her sister glow with such happiness. 'Billy and I have been trying for a while. I've miscarried twice in the first trimester but I'm determined to hang on to this one.'

'Ah…the power of positive thinking. Just as well you have young Robby to look after you, too. I'm looking forward to meeting him…if he ever wakes up.'

Aracely smiled and looked at the clock on the wall and moaned, feeling suddenly tired. 'Half past two? Is that really the time?'

'Sure is.' Maggie yawned.

'Go and get some rest.' Aracely placed her hand on her sister's shoulder, hoping Mags would listen to her.

'You know I don't sleep when Billy's out on these sorts of rescues. I know he loves going, he gets such an adrenaline buzz and he's good at what he does, but…' Maggie trailed off, her hand rubbing her stomach yet again.

'You're his wife, Mags. It's only natural you should be worried. Billy will call as soon as he can.' Aracely knew she sounded a lot more sure than she really was, but she had to bolster her sister's spirits. 'At least go and put your feet up.

On the sofa, or go lie down with Robby in my bed. You know how he loves to snuggle.'

'He also loves to kick. I'll take the sofa, that way it'll be easier to get up should I be needed.'

The SES radio she carried crackled to life and both women jumped at the sound. 'Honey?' Billy called.

'I'm here.'

'Yeah, we're gonna need Aracely's help, darl. Winston Chapman's house has collapsed and he's stuck inside. We're diggin' him out now but I don't know what sort of shape he's gonna be in.'

Aracely nodded. 'Tell him I'm on my way.'

Maggie relayed the message and Aracely headed out and down to her consulting room. She'd just started to let her mind and body relax and now she had to pump it up again. Standing in the middle of the room, she closed her eyes, mentally thinking through what she might find on arrival at Mr Chapman's house and what supplies she would need to take with her. Her neck cricked as she moved and she groaned, bringing her right hand up to massage the tired muscles as best she could.

'Here. Allow me.' Trent came up behind her

and before she could protest he'd brushed her hand aside and moved her hair out of the way. It was still tied back in a ponytail but little tendrils, small dark curls, had escaped and as he smoothed them away she shivered at the touch, her senses rising to fever pitch.

She gulped, so aware of him, so conscious of his body close to hers once more. 'I'm sorry if my fingers are still a little cool.' His warm words fanned her neck and she accepted the tingles that spread through her body.

'Oh, it's OK.' Her voice had taken on a dreamy quality as she tried not to moan out loud as his nimble fingers kneaded gently in the exact spot, but it was difficult to resist. 'Mmm. That's it.' Aracely couldn't believe how incredible it felt, his hands easing the pain, endorphins being released, making her light-headed and her muscles relax.

Her heart, though, was pounding loudly against her chest and she could hear it reverberating in her ears. They were in their own little bubble. Just the two of them, Trent's hands working magic on her neck and taut trapezius muscles.

'You're really very tight,' he murmured, his voice low and intimate.

'It's where I put all my stress,' she whispered back. It was almost impossible for her to open her eyes now, such was the splendour of his hands working their magic on her exhausted body. Her head rolled back and he shifted to accommodate it, and before Aracely could move, could regain control over her senses, she realised he was letting her lean her head on his shoulder, his fingers still kneading gently but methodically.

She didn't notice when they slowed and eventually stopped. Her breathing was now deep, her heart now at a decent resting rate, and all the tension that had coursed through her with the night's events seemed to drain out in a pool at her feet. She was now leaning against him, his hands sliding down from her shoulders to rest around her elbows.

'Mmm,' she breathed. 'You have magic fingers.'

Trent gulped, wishing she didn't sound so delectable, her voice low and seductive. Helping her out with a brief massage had been all he'd intended, but when she'd started turning to putty beneath his hands he'd found himself moving closer, wanting her to relax, and now she was practically limp against him, her back pressed to his chest.

He breathed in, her hair smelling of sweet spices and perfume, which was an intoxicating combination as their body heat began to mingle. Since his disastrous marriage, Trent had kept his distance where women were concerned, but he'd never met anyone like Aracely before. She was amazing and the more time he spent with her, the more he continued to realise how incredible she was, not just as a doctor but as a woman. Now, as he almost held her in his arms, he was beginning to think this chemistry that had seemed to spring from nowhere to engulf them both was something he shouldn't simply dismiss.

He'd fallen quickly into marriage with Tessa and had vowed if he *ever* contemplated a serious relationship again that he'd take his time, that he'd explore all the angles, yet, standing here with Aracely, he could feel himself forgetting all his sage advice and plans. It felt good having her so close, feeling her so relaxed against him. He also knew it was a moment—just a moment—stolen in the midst of what was turning out to be the busiest night of his life, and sometimes those stolen moments were the best. He didn't want to break it but one of them had to be in control and as she felt as though she was almost asleep on her feet, he realised it fell to him to be the bearer of logic.

'Aracely?'

'Shh.' She frowned. 'Don't talk,' she whispered.

Trent's lips tugged into a little smile and as he shifted her slightly, he placed his hands at her waist, supporting her in case her legs gave way and she fell to the floor. He could now look into her face and as her eyes slowly fluttered open he swallowed at the vulnerability he saw there. The smile slid away as he glanced from her eyes to her mouth and back again. She was close, she was willing—that much he could tell—but he also knew both of them would have regrets later. Fatigue and stress were definitely taking their toll on both of them. Carefully, he led her to the chair behind her desk and held onto her until she was sitting.

Extracting himself, he turned and took a few steps away, desperate now to get himself back under control. He could have kissed her, kissed this woman he hardly knew, and that was enough to shake his well-ordered world. He was a doctor, a professional and temporary colleague there to help Aracely...temporary being the operative word. He'd initially come down to her consulting room to offer his services for whatever she was heading off to face. How had things got out of control so quickly? Trent raked a hand through his hair and worked to pull himself together.

'OK.' Aracely finally spoke and he heard her drag in a not-so-steady breath. 'Back to reality. I'm going to need bandages, probably a saline drip and Winston Chapman's file, although I don't think he's allergic to anything.'

Trent turned and looked at her as she stood and crossed to the filing cabinet in the corner. She hunted through it to find the file on her patient and scanned it briefly. 'I can help,' he stated, and her eyes flicked up to look at him for a long moment.

'Sure.' With that she simply handed him the file and closed the cabinet, before opening a cupboard on the back wall and started pulling out the things she needed. She found another backpack, this one without a cross, but she bundled everything into it, packing it neatly and speaking softly to herself as she did so.

Trent watched her for a moment, wondering whether he'd imagined her earlier reaction. Had he been the only one who'd felt it? No. He dismissed that thought. He knew what he'd seen in Aracely's eyes. The moment they'd just shared hadn't been the only one since they'd met, the heightened awareness of one another growing with each encounter. She was simply doing her job, staying focused and getting ready to head out into the storm once more.

'What do you need me to do?'

'A final check on your friends would be good. Leave Maggie some instructions but remember that I want her off her feet for as much as possible. Hopefully, we'll only be about an hour or two at the absolute worst. We won't be able to transfer anyone to Moonta hospital tonight or even tomorrow, depending on when this rain lets up. Anyway, if Greg, Phil and Dan are all stable and Maggie only needs to do simple observations while we're gone, that would be good. Any more than that and you'll need to stay here with them. I'll not have Maggie risking her baby when she doesn't need to.'

Trent nodded. 'Agreed. Dan's quite coherent and it's only his knee that is busted. He can keep a pretty close eye on the guys.'

'Good.' With a brief nod Trent left her small consulting room and Aracely was hard pressed not to collapse back into the chair. My goodness! What on earth had happened between them? It was dangerous, it was exciting and it was starting to become real the more time she spent with him. 'You need to maintain stronger control,' she lectured herself as she finished packing her bag and went to check on Robby.

She sighed with a smile, seeing him lying there, the blankets crumpled and messy all around his little body. So delicious, so gorgeous, so peaceful. How she wished she could join him. Instead, she turned, headed to her wardrobe and pulled out another wet-weather coat and then her bright orange SES jacket which she put over the top.

'Mummy?'

She turned and headed over to the bed. 'Shh, darling. Go back to sleep.'

'Is someone hurt?'

'Yes. Aunty Maggie's here to look after you.' Aracely soothed the hair away from his face, realising he was a little cool.

'I'm in your bed?' he asked.

'Yes. You keep it warm for me.' She pulled the blankets up, straightening them before bending to kiss him. 'Back to sleep, now. OK? Mummy loves you.'

'Love you too, Mummy,' he mumbled, and snuggled in, sleep already claiming him once more. When she turned, she realised Trent was standing in her open doorway and she automatically raised a finger to her lips, indicating he should be quiet. He nodded and as she slipped out, closing the door behind her, she let out a deep sigh.

'He woke up?' Trent asked as she headed to the lounge room.

'Only for a moment. He'll be fine.'

'Good.' Seeing Aracely with her son brought back the loss of the child he didn't have. His wife had a daughter—a four-year-old daughter—but he wasn't the father.

After checking Maggie and making sure she was comfortable, Aracely gathered her bag and SES radio and looked at Trent. 'Ready?'

'As I'll ever be.'

'OK. Let's go.' When they stepped outside, the rain hit them full in the face once more. 'And we're back,' Aracely joked as she rushed to her four-wheel-drive, wondering how long it would take for her to become drenched this time. At least she was dry to start off with and so was Trent. As he climbed into her car, she noticed the boots he'd been wearing before and grimaced. 'Wet feet already, Dr Mornington?'

'Wet shoes equals wet feet, Dr Smith, but as it's all that's on offer, I'll take it. Borrowed clothes I'm fine with, but I doubt Billy has the same sized feet as me.' He shrugged as though he wasn't really bothered about having to wear wet shoes. 'Let's get to this new accident site and get the show on the road.'

'Excellent suggestion,' she said, started the engine and reversed out of the driveway. Using the electronic gear selector, she took the car out of Reverse and switched it into Drive.

'I like your car modifications,' Trent said a few minutes later as she drove along the black road, the car's headlights illuminating the rain, which was coming down at an angle. 'Especially the steering knob.'

'It allows total one-handed control. I can change gears with my left hand, hold the steering-wheel and things like that, but not for extended periods of time. Took a while to get used to but, as I've said, it's amazing the way the brain compensates for changes.'

Within a few minutes they were there. 'That was quick,' Trent commented as she slowed the car to crawl along the street, which was littered with tree branches and other debris.

'This isn't Sydney, Trent.' She parked the car and reached into the back for her bag. Glancing around at what she saw, she shook her head. 'What a night.'

They climbed out and Trent stayed close as Aracely led the way to where other men in the same orange vests she wore were huddled together talking under a makeshift canopy at the edge of the road.

'Here she is,' Billy called and beckoned them over. 'Trent. Good on ya, mate.' Trent found his hand being shaken heartily by Billy. 'Told ya we'd make a rescuer out of you.' Billy handed Trent a spare orange SES jacket. 'Put this on. Well, look at that. Perfect fit.'

'Don't get any ideas. I'm just here to help.' Trent laughed.

'What's the situation?' Aracely asked.

'Winston's gone and got himself pinned,' Billy said. 'The tree across the road came down right in the middle of his house. He'd have had little warning but we've been able to ascertain he's alive and OK. Said his hands are in a bad way but, apart from that, he just can't move. Kieran and his men are having a turn at shifting the debris. We've been taking it in turns so we don't get too tired. The usual.'

'You can't get any heavy machinery in to lift beams?' Trent asked.

'Too risky. Too unstable,' Aracely replied.

'Hey!' There was a shout in the distance and

in the next instant Billy's radio came to life. 'Billy, we need you,' Kieran, the SES chief, said, and Billy headed out into the rain once more. He returned a few minutes later and nodded to Aracely and Trent. 'You're on.'

Carefully, they followed Billy and, unlike the beach rescue, there were large spotlights all over the place, illuminating the area. 'We've managed to shift the top part off and you can get to Winston now. Not his legs, though. We'll need to keep digging him out but if you can assess him, give him something for the pain, that sort of thing, it'd be bonza,' Billy instructed, and Aracely nodded.

'He's conscious?'

'Too right.' Billy grinned with delight. She concentrated on carefully following in Billy's footsteps but his step was bigger than hers, the wind and rain combining to make it very difficult. Aracely stumbled but instantly found Trent's hands at her waist, steadying her.

'Thanks,' she tossed over her shoulder, and had to struggle against the warmth his touch left behind. It was the last thing she needed at the moment but she guessed it was better than falling over and injuring herself in the process.

'You need to crawl through here,' Billy said, and crouched down to squeeze through a small opening.

'Give me the bag,' Trent said, lifting the backpack from her shoulders. 'You go through and then I can pass it to you.'

'Sure.' Aracely did as he'd suggested and went down on all fours to crawl through the small area which usually led into Mr Chapman's living room. 'I can't believe this,' she said to herself as she came out the other side. At least in this part of the house the roof was still on and therefore provided them with a bit of shelter. She reached around to take the medical bag and couldn't help the grin as Trent squeezed his tall frame through the small space.

'This way,' Billy called beckoning them over. 'He's this way.'

The wooden floor boards of Winston Chapman's home were now littered with broken ornaments, photographs, smashed glass from windows and broken plates. The devastation was acute. Finally, when they reached their patient, Aracely gasped and rushed to his side. He was lying down, only his upper torso visible to them, a roof beam pinned across his legs.

'Winston!' Aracely knelt down, glad the wind and rain couldn't reach them there. Her hands were wet but that didn't stop her from touching his face with care. He was covered in scratches and bruises but his hands were the worst as he lifted them up. 'How are you holding up?' she asked.

'I've been better, Doc.'

'But your legs?'

'They're not broken, just pinned,' Billy reported. Trent had knelt down beside Aracely and was opening the backpack. 'We've wrapped his hands up, tried to stop the bleeding and stuff, but we'll let you take a good look at them.'

'Are you in any pain?' Aracely asked Winston as she felt his pulse. Trent handed her a stethoscope and she immediately listened to her patient's chest.

'My hands are numb, Doc.'

'OK. I think we'll give you some morphine so we're ready to move you once Kieran and his team get that beam off your legs.' When it was time to unwrap his hands, which were covered with a very crude temporary dressing, Aracely shook her head. 'How on earth did your hands get this bad?' There were several lacerations as well as broken skin and busted fingernails, not to mention all the splinters.

'I was buried, Doc. Started to claw my way out and got this far when that stuff shifted and pinned me. At least then I could breathe more easily.'

Aracely simply shook her head in concerned astonishment before turning to Trent. 'What's his BP?'

'Fine,' Trent replied, removing the portable blood-pressure cuff.

'Billy's given me tea, keeping my fluids up,' said Winston. ' I feel OK. Shaken but OK, Doc.'

'You've been incredibly lucky, Winston.'

'That I have, Doc.'

'Dr Mornington and I will debride the areas as best we can and get sterile dressings on. That's about all I can do for now but I think it's more important to get you settled for the night a.s.a.p. and then tomorrow we'll be able to take a closer look and really see what the damage is.' She shook her head again before they began work, Trent pre-empting her beautifully.

'Billy?' she called as Trent finished off the bandage on the left hand. 'I'll need some plastic bags. When we move him, I don't want these dressings getting wet.'

'Righto, Cely.' With that, her brother-in-law disappeared but returned a few minutes later with what she'd requested.

'OK, listen up, people,' Kieran called. 'Now that the medics have done their job, we're gonna finish cutting this beam in half and get it off Winston once and for all.' A cheer went up, Winston joining in. Billy escorted Aracely and Trent back to the shelter before heading back to join his team.

'Looks like it's just the two of us,' Trent remarked as he put the bag on the ground.

'We've done our bit. Now we're in the way.' Aracely smiled but it didn't quite reach her eyes.

'What will you do once they've managed to get Winston out?'

'That's what I'm trying to think through. My

place is full to the brim and I can't get him to the hospital.'

'What about the neighbours?' Trent looked around at the other houses in the street, amazed that all the other houses were still standing.

'Mrs Edmonson lives next door. I'm sure she'll be able to put Winston up for the night. I'll sort something else out tomorrow when I've had time to think.'

'And sleep.'

'Yes. Sleep is good.' Aracely kept looking towards where she could hear the chainsaw being operated, trying not to grimace.

'Were you trapped in the car?' Trent asked softly.

'Pardon?'

'When you had your injury. Were you trapped in the car?'

'Yes. Five hours it took to get me out.'

'Jaws of life?'

'You guessed it.' She nodded and looked down at her crippled hand.

'Do you think about it much?'

'Nope. The first few years were difficult but that's to be expected when dealing with multiple

trauma. Now…' She shrugged. 'I'm just me. I
have a bad hand, everyone accepts that. It doesn't
define me.'

Trent's admiration for her increased another
notch. 'You're so different.'

'Pardon?'

'From other women. You're so different.'

'Is that a good thing?'

'Most definitely.' He nodded for emphasis.
'Admirable, too.'

She shrugged again. 'Life goes on.' She looked
at him as she spoke and in the midst of the
battery-operated light which lit the small shelter
she thought she saw pain flit across his features,
touching his eyes and making them more solemn
than she'd ever seen them.

'That it does,' he agreed quietly.

CHAPTER FIVE

THE silence that seemed to surround them was punctured by a cheer of delight from the SES team and soon they were able to bring Winston out. Aracely and Trent examined him and pronounced his hands the worst of his injuries. Before they left, Aracely made sure her patient was settled in Mrs Edmonson's spare room, the neighbourly woman chatting and gasping with horror at the night's events.

'It's just horrible, Dr Smith. Simply horrible. But don't you worry about Winston. I'll take good care of him and you say you'll be around tomorrow so that'll be just fine, but rest assured that Winston's more than welcome to stay as long as you think he needs to be here. I'll cope just fine. I was the one who raised the alarm, you know. I heard this awful noise and honestly I thought the sky was falling, but when I went to investigate by looking out my window, oh, Dr Smith, I was fluttering and trembling all over but I called the emergency number and thankfully my phone hadn't been disconnected so I was able to get through and get help to poor Winston.' Emily Edmonson barely paused for breath as she chattered on, but eventually she finally finished her tale. 'Now, Dr Smith, don't you worry about Winston here. I'll take excellent care of him and see you later on. Off you go now.'

Aracely thanked the elderly lady and said goodbye before heading back to check in with Kieran, only to find him chatting with Trent and Billy, all of them laughing. 'If you don't need me any more, Kieran, I think I'll head home.'

'Go, Aracely. Trent's checked the men over and pronounced them all ready for sleep so we'll just finish up here and then return once the sun's up and hopefully the rain's stopped, or at least not pelting down so hard and consistently,' Kieran replied.

'Thanks.' She turned to her brother-in-law. 'Mags isn't going to leave my house until you're home so don't be too long.'

'Right behind you, Cely,' Billy replied, and crossed his heart in a promise.

'Good. Trent?'

'Ready when you are,' he said, heaving the backpack on.

''Night, all,' she said, and didn't bother to respond when everyone told her it was really early morning. 'As far as I'm concerned, it's still night. It won't be morning until I've had some sleep,' she muttered as they walked down the street to her car. 'You'll need to talk to me while I drive, Trent. Keep me awake.'

'Of course,' he agreed and did so, chatting about nothing in particular. When his stomach growled, he quickly apologised.

'Don't worry. I think mine's about to growl in sympathy. Maggie had soup on before and I'm sure there'll be plenty left.'

'I've heard about your sister's cooking.'

'Then you'll have to sample some. Besides, full tummies will help us sleep better.'

Trent chuckled.

'What's so funny?'

'Full tummy. You sound just like a mother.'

'That's because I am one.'

'Your son's important to you?'

Aracely was taken aback at the question. 'Of course he is. He's my world.' She shook her head. 'That's a strange question to ask, Trent.'

'Not really.'

Aracely held her breath for a moment, wondering whether she should ask him about his personal life. His last statement had revealed a lot about him or about someone he knew. Did he know someone whose children weren't important to them? Could she ask? He'd certainly probed into her life but if she probed into his, she'd probably find him far too interesting and then have even more difficulty saying goodbye to him when the time came, which it inevitably would. 'Do *you* have children?' she ventured, and instantly wanted to take it back when his head jerked around sharply to look at her.

'No.'

'Married?'

'No.'

'Never found the right woman or just not time yet?' What a dumb question, she thought, and rolled her eyes, but the growing need inside her to know more about this man was what had propelled her forward.

He was silent for so long that she was about to apologise for prying when he said, 'I thought I had—found the right woman, that is.'

'Didn't work out?'

'No. We divorced the same year as you. Five years ago.'

'Ah. We said it wasn't a good year.' She smiled sadly. 'I'm sorry.'

'For?'

'Any time a marriage ends, it isn't good. I'm sorry things didn't work out for you.'

'Just as you're sorry they didn't work out between you and your ex-husband?'

'Exactly, but we're human, we make mistakes. However, it's what we do with those mistakes that makes us better humans.'

'Profound.'

She laughed as she pulled into her driveway and switched off the engine. 'I wish I could take credit for it. My mother says that. Very wise woman, my mum.'

'I'm sorry I'll miss meeting her.'

Aracely turned to face him and nodded. 'So am I,' she said softly. 'She would have liked you.'

'Oh?' He seemed surprised. 'What makes you say that?'

'You're a man of action, Trent. A man of principle. You rescued your three friends tonight, putting your own life in danger time and time again, but you did it. You had a goal and you achieved it.' She shrugged. 'That either takes a lot of guts or a lot of stupidity.'

'Or a lot of both.' He chuckled and she agreed. When his stomach growled again, Aracely pulled the key from the ignition.

'Let's go eat.'

'Sounds like a plan.'

'Then I'll look at your leg.' She didn't wait for a response and instead grabbed her bag and headed indoors, leaving him to follow. Without a word, they both separated, Trent to check on his friends and Aracely to check on her son and sister. Robby was once more tangled in the blankets but this time his skin was warm to her touch. She ran her hand across the dark mop of curls he'd inherited from her before going to check on Maggie. Her sister was snuggled up on the sofa, the home-made quilt Maggie had stitched last year as a Christmas present for Robby draped over her body to keep her warm. The fire had started to die down and Aracely automatically stoked it before making her way to the kitchen.

'Hi,' she said, finding Trent there, stirring the soup on the stove. 'How are your friends?'

'Good. Dan said that both Greg and Phil have regained consciousness, which is excellent news. Phil's BP is stable and his sleep is more restful than restless.'

'Good to hear. And Dan?'

'Oh he's fine. Painkillers are still working and the bandage on his knee is helping to keep it im-mobilised for now.' As he spoke, Aracely watched him open cupboards, finding two bowls and cutlery. Her kitchen was a long, thin rectan-gle and although more than enough for one person, it was difficult to fit two fully grown adults side by side without them brushing up against each other, which was why she was more than happy to have Trent poking about in her cupboards.

The gas burners didn't take long to heat the soup and soon he was dishing it out, carrying both bowls to the dining-room table where they spoke in soft tones so as not to wake Maggie.

'Mmm, this is delicious.' Trent sipped at the liquid on his spoon.

'It's our mother's recipe but whenever I make it, it never turns out as good as this.' She sighed. 'Maggie inherited all the domestic skills, cooking, sewing and such. I'm no good at them.'

'Instead you inherited…what?'

'Medicine, I guess. My dad was a doctor.'

'Was?'

'Retired now, which is why they're taking the opportunity to travel, see a bit of the world. The last postcard we received was from Prague.'

'Good for them.' Trent's enthusiasm was heartfelt. 'Was he an outback GP like you?'

'We're hardly outback, Trent. The Yorke Peninsula is probably considered rural but not outback, although if you travelled north for a day or two, you'd certainly hit the middle of Australia.'

'Ever been?'

'To the real outback?'

'Yes.'

Aracely nodded. 'I did six months there before I decided to head to the city and try my hand at a surgical speciality.' She laughed and looked down at her crippled fingers. 'Instead I tried my hand at surviving an accident.'

'You certainly have a positive outlook on what happened.'

'Is there any other? Getting depressed, letting it get to you, doesn't help with anything. Sure, there are days when I resent what happened but then I stop and consider how I might have ended up losing my arm altogether or, worse, my life.' Aracely shrugged. 'The brain is an amazing organ and it doesn't take long for it to retrain itself. I know I sound like a broken record when I keep saying that, but it's true. I'm so in awe of how my body just does things, compensates, and it's as though my brain has worked it all out and is teaching me how to cope.'

'Wow. You should come and give a lecture to some of my patients. They've been in bad accidents and although their bodies heal, their minds take a lot longer.'

'Clinical studies have proven that having a positive attitude towards trauma only enhances survival and healing rates.'

'Can't argue with that,' Trent added, finishing off his soup. 'Mmm. Delicious. I'll have to remember to tell Maggie how much I enjoyed her cooking.'

Aracely agreed. 'You do that. She loves getting compliments. I think sometimes she feels as though she doesn't really do anything. She's the home-maker and I'm the one who saves people's lives—well, usually I do.'

Trent nodding, knowing exactly what she was talking about. 'Maggie feels inferior?'

'I don't know if inferior is the right word but when we were younger she kept wanting to know what she was good at. What could she do with her life. I was always off with my dad, helping him on his house calls, dissecting dead animals.' She shrugged. 'That sort of thing. Yet Maggie loved cooking and being at home and making things. Now, though, I think she realises she's the glue. She keeps me afloat, she's always there for Billy.

Both of us have demanding jobs yet without a strong support team or backbone, we'd both come apart at the seams. Besides, she is going to make the best mother. Robby's so excited about having a cousin—*at last,*' she said, with the same emphasis her son usually put on the words.

Trent watched her intently as she spoke, seeing the natural bond the two sisters shared. 'It's good that you two live so close.'

'Yes. I love having her near.'

'It's nice to see.' Trent toyed with his spoon for a moment and she watched him closely.

'What about your parents?' she asked, hoping they hadn't passed away.

His eyes met hers and she paused, spoon raised halfway to her lips. It was as though she was issuing a challenge, asking him to tell her a bit about himself. 'I'm not trying to pry, Trent,' she tried to reassure him. 'Just making conversation. If you have trouble talking about your family, that's fine. Ignore my questions or tell me to mind my own business. I guess I don't mind talking about my family because they're simply so much a part of me—of us—Robby and me, I mean.'

Trent nodded. 'That's obvious.' He glanced across at where Maggie still slept. 'It's…comforting to see a family so close, to see sisters working together side by side and helping each other, the way you and Maggie do.'

'Do you have siblings?'

'I do.' He leaned back in his chair. 'I come from a very large family. Lots of aunts and uncles, cousins, nieces and nephews and I have four brothers and two sisters.'

'Wow.'

'That's what I say.'

'Do they live close?'

'My immediate family is mostly in Sydney, one sister is in Queensland, and I have two brothers in Melbourne so they're not far.'

'So you see them quite regularly?'

'For the most part.' He was still being tight-lipped, although she couldn't help shake the feeling that he wanted to say more. 'Every month there are several birthday parties happening but…' He took in a breath and slowly exhaled. 'But since my divorce I don't usually go.'

She raised her eyebrows at this telling piece of

information. 'Oh. Well, it's difficult with shift work and patients needing attention at all hours—as has been proven tonight.'

'This morning,' he corrected, and she was pleased to see a small smile touch his lips.

'I've told you, it won't be morning until I've slept.' She looked up at the old clock sitting on her bookshelf and groaned.

'What's wrong?'

'Robby. He's usually up early. I'll probably be able to manage a few hours' sleep and then it'll be time for the morning routine.'

'At least he's slept through most of the storm and you didn't have to deal with a scared child as well as strange men pounding on your door.' Again his lips twitched and she was glad to see him smiling. It was obvious he had some deep-seated problems with his family which were somehow tied into his divorce but although she was more than willing to talk about her life and past history, it appeared Trent wasn't. He was perfectly within his rights. He was an interesting man and she was now sorry she wouldn't have the opportunity to get to know him better. They all knew that once the storm lifted and the creek receded, Trent and his friends would be able to head back to their lives in Sydney, doing what they did best, and their eventful fishing trip to the Yorke Peninsula would be an interesting story they could tell to all their friends and colleagues.

Aracely sighed and it was then she realised she was simply sitting there, staring across the table at Trent. The odd thing was, he was sitting there, staring back, the smile having slipped from his lips.

'Don't try and figure me out, Aracely,' he said softly. 'I'm a complex man.'

'You don't need to be. Life can be simple if you take the time to weed out all the junk and focus on what's really important.'

He leaned forward putting his elbows on the table and propping his chin on his hands. 'You've been through a lot.'

'I have.'

He searched her eyes and she let him, let him see whatever he wanted to see. Finally he said, 'You give me hope.'

'Hope?'

'That my life can one day be simple, too, because right now it seems so complicated.'

'Is it really, though? Or is it just that you're looking more at the forest than the trees?'

Trent shook his head sadly then shrugged. 'Sometimes I don't have a clue what I'm doing. At the moment, I still feel that I'm in survival mode.'

'That does tend to last for a while but it does pass. You move from feeling as though you're constantly in winter, through to a glorious spring and before you know it, summer is shining down on you.'

'How long did it take for you?'

'Ah, I can't go giving you that answer,' she said with a smile. 'It's different for everyone. I will, however, say that you need a support team. They're vital. If you don't have that, if you don't have people you can talk to, people you can trust and lean on, then your winter may last quite a bit longer. After my accident and the subsequent break-up of my marriage, my family formed a tight unit around me, helping and protecting me from further hurts.' Her smile increased. 'And then I had Robby and although I was physically still stuck in winter, having operations on my hand and physiotherapy and all that stuff, I was emotionally in summer because he brought such love into my life.'

Trent slowly nodded, the pain piercing him. He'd missed out on that, Tessa ripping away his right to parenthood.

Aracely held her hand out and he tentatively put his into hers. Her hand was warm, her skin smooth to the touch, sending tingles up and down his arm. 'Find your support team, Trent. That's the first step. Find people who will help you, people you feel comfortable leaning on. They don't have to be family, just people you know.' She paused and looked into his eyes, seeing the sorrow there. 'You've already been in winter far too long.'

'Know me well, do you?'

'I can see it. I can hear it in your voice and I can recognise it because I've been there, too. Besides, after what we've been through together in the past eight hours…' She sighed. 'It feels as though we've squashed a lifetime into them.'

He nodded slowly, agreeing with her. Aracely gave his hand a little squeeze. 'Search for your spring and, I guarantee you, you'll find it sooner than you think.'

'You really believe that?'

'I not only believe it, I'm living proof it works.' She waited, still holding his hand. Trent looked into her compassionate brown eyes and for the first time he could remember found himself wanting to unburden a little.

'My wife had an affair,' he stated, his voice calm. 'I bore the brunt of the blame, from both Tessa and my family. Finding people I trust, people I can talk to, isn't easy for me, Aracely. Dan, Phil and Greg are my closest friends and while I know they support me...' He shook his head. 'We don't really talk or open up to each other. It's not that sort of friendship.'

She nodded. 'I can understand that. They're friends but they're also colleagues.'

'Exactly.' She *did* understand.

When the front door opened suddenly, Aracely jumped, letting go of Trent's hand and jerking to her feet, her heart pounding as Billy walked in. He looked at his sister-in-law. 'Sorry, Cely. Trent.' He nodded. 'Didn't mean to scare you.' He walked over to the sofa and looked down at his wife, a smile warming his face. 'I'll take her home.'

Aracely started clearing the table. 'We're just heading off to bed, too.'

'Everything settled at Mr Chapman's house?' Trent asked. Aracely didn't hear Billy's muffled answer as she stacked the dishes in the dishwasher, still trying to come to terms with the intimacy she'd shared with Trent. He'd been hurt, that much was evident, and she sincerely hoped her words were enough to help him through.

A bond had formed between them tonight and the discussion they'd just had had only increased that bond. She wasn't sure how or when they'd become friends but she felt as though that was exactly what they were, and now she found herself wishing he could stay longer, that they could spend more time together, that he could meet Robby. Robby would be so good for Trent. Her son had a gift for making people happy and he did it just by being himself.

She realised Billy was ready to leave and headed out to say goodnight to him and her sleepy sister as he carried his wife out into the

darkness of the morning. After she'd shut the
door behind them, she turned to face Trent. He
was standing there, wet shoes off, a dry pair of
socks on his feet and his hands shoved into the
pockets of the borrowed jeans.

'I take it I'm sleeping out here?' Trent said and
pointed to the sofa.

'Yes. I keep it made up but I'll get you some
extra blankets.'

He nodded and when he crossed to the sofa,
she remembered his sore leg.

'Oh, I'll get the bandages for your leg as well.'
Before he could say a word, she headed to her
clinic room to collect the bandages, checking on
all of their patients as she went. Thankfully, all
three were sleeping and she noted the impro-
vised traction Trent had obviously rigged up to
keep Phil's pelvic fracture as stable as possible.

Aracely returned to the lounge room where
Trent had pulled out the sofa-bed and was
standing by the fire, side on to her, his eyes closed.
It was as though he was asleep on his feet and she
didn't blame him one bit. The man had been
through so much and he was lucky to be alive.

Different scenarios, things that might have gone wrong with the rescue of his friends, flashed through her mind in a maze of pictures and she shuddered, pushing them aside. Nothing had gone wrong. Trent was all right. *All* of them were all right and she was thankful for that sweet miracle.

Trent yawned, stretching out his tired muscles, pushing his arms high above his head, and she stood stock-still, completely enthralled by the sight of him. He rolled his neck, then bent slowly from side to side. She realised just how small the borrowed clothes he was wearing really were on him as the shirt and jumper rode up and his trousers dipped down, giving her a glorious sneak peek of his firm and sculptured abdomen. No wonder this man had been able to get through what he had tonight, he was in prime physical condition.

When an unbidden sigh escaped her lips, his eyes snapped open and his gaze met hers. He slowly lowered his arms, his clothing shifting back into place to hide her view. Aracely was powerless to look away, to deny the effect he was having on her. Whoever this man was, he was trouble. She should be panicking, trying to get away but instead she stood her ground, drowning in those glorious brown eyes of his.

Her tongue darted out to wet her lips and she wasn't at all sure what to do or say next. She'd just ogled a man—a man she hardly knew—and although the evening they'd shared had been dramatic and highly intense, that wasn't any excuse for her behaviour. Yet all she could do was stay exactly where she was and hug the blanket tighter to her chest, waiting for him to speak, to say something—anything.

'It's OK to look, Aracely.' His tone was soft and deep, his eyes encompassing her, warming her through and through. The arrogance of his words penetrated her mind but it wasn't quite enough to make her move. 'Never any harm in looking.'

As he spoke, he looked down at her parted lips, the action causing longing to flood through her. Was he playing games? Did he feel the same attraction she felt for him? It was true that she'd caught him looking at her a few times during the evening's events but she'd dismissed it. Had she read the signals incorrectly? Could she actually believe that this irresistible, sexy man found *her* attractive?

His eyes then dipped lower, travelling down her body in a slow and intimate visual caress. Her stomach churned and warmth flooded through her as he finally looked into her eyes once more. He shook his head slowly. 'Then again…' His tone was deep and she could hear the desire in it. 'Perhaps I was wrong. Perhaps there *is* harm in looking because it can so easily turn into something else.'

'Something else?' she squeaked, and her nervousness must have been evident in her features because Trent slowly covered the distance between them. Aracely knew she should move, should say something, do something to stop him before he reached her, but she was powerless, caught up in his magnetism, transfixed like an animal caught in beam of a car's headlights.

'Yes.'

Her heart was pounding wildly against her chest as he came nearer and she found herself hypnotised. He stopped walking, coming to stand just in front of her. Aracely stared at him, her grip tightening on the items she had clutched to her chest. Without a word and without breaking eye contact, Trent reached out and gently brushed a curl that had escaped her band back behind her ear. Strangely, there didn't seem to be any need to say anything, both of them locked in a suspended moment in time.

She couldn't believe how such a simple action, a simple touch could totally rock her world. Everything she knew, everything she'd studied and experienced during her life seemed to literally tilt from side to side. Who was this man and how could his touch make her heart race, her breath catch and her head spin?

Something new and exciting yet dangerous was enveloping them and Aracely wasn't at all sure what she should do about it. She sighed, still unable to look away. His eyes were so amazingly deep and reassuring. It was as though he wanted her to know he wouldn't harm her. Instinctively, she believed him, especially after what had happened that night.

'Aracely.' Her name was a caress on his lips and his fingers trailed down her neck, his hand coming to rest on her shoulder. The sigh that escaped her ended up more as a groan, only serving to intensify the moment they were sharing. Trent couldn't believe how exquisite she was. He opened his mouth to tell her but the words seemed to stick in his throat and he knew that even if he said them, she wouldn't believe him.

Aracely had already told him she'd been hurt once before. That she'd taken a gamble on love and she'd lost. Although she exhibited self-confidence, he also knew she was highly conscious of her disability and where it didn't bother him in the slightest, if he were to touch her hand or stroke it, he wondered if she would pull away.

She was brave and he wasn't just thinking about the way she'd helped him rescue his friends that evening. No, this woman, this special woman had hidden depths. She'd been knocked down but she'd risen above it, to find a better life, and he admired her courage. He could learn from her.

Aracely looked at his lips as he breathed her name again, then back to his eyes. Was he simply saying her name or was he asking a question? Asking her whether it was all right for him to invade her personal space, to touch her…to kiss her? If that was the case, how should she answer? Did she want him to kiss her? She found it difficult to believe he'd want that, but then again after everything she'd felt when they'd been alone like this, the way he'd almost touched her several times, the things he'd said—it was all evidence to the contrary. *Go for it,* a voice said from deep within her, urging her on.

'Yes?' The single word was forced past her lips and came out as a breathy whisper, and she instantly hoped she wasn't making a huge mistake. If he hadn't been seeking permission, she might be about to make a complete fool of herself.

Trent searched her face for a moment longer, his hand cupping her chin as he tilted it slightly, then began to close the remaining distance between them, leaning in closer, his head making its excruciatingly slow descent.

Aracely's heart started beating in triple time as she realised she'd interpreted all the signals correctly. How had this happened? Why was it happening? He was a stranger, someone she'd only met a few hours ago. It was the road to heartbreak and she was actually about to take the first step onto the bitumen. Still, she couldn't move. She was completely captivated. Transfixed.

CHAPTER SIX

'Mummy!' Robby's wail broke through the haze that surrounded them both, and Aracely jerked back, rushing from the room, unsure of why she was reacting to Trent the way she was.

'I'm here,' she said as she hurried to where Robby was sitting up in bed. 'What's wrong?'

'I had a bad dream, Mummy.' As she brushed a hand over his hair and face, she felt his cheeks were a little damp.

'Oh, honey. It's all right.' She kissed away his tears. 'Mummy's here. I'm right here.' He was wide awake now and she wondered whether she'd be able to get him back to sleep at all. 'Every thing's OK, baby.'

'I'm not a baby,' he returned.

'No. Of course. I didn't mean it like that. Sometimes the word baby also means darling.'

'Oh.' Robby hugged her close, then asked quite calmly, 'Who's that man?'

Aracely turned quickly and saw Trent standing in the doorway.

'I didn't mean to intrude,' he instantly apologised. 'Just wanted to make sure everyone was OK.'

'Robby had a bad dream.' Aracely shifted on the bed and beckoned Trent in. 'Robby, this is Dr Mornington.'

He smiled at the little boy. 'Call me Trent.'

'Why?'

'Because that's my name.' He stopped in front of the bed and held out his hand in greeting. Robby was delighted to shake hands with him in a grown-up fashion. 'Some of my friends and I were in a bit of an accident tonight and your mummy has been working very hard to make sure we're all better.'

'Do you have a sore leg?' Robby freed himself from his mother's hold and switched on the bedside light, making the two adults blink in the sudden brightness.

'Yes, he does,' Aracely replied. 'I was just about to fix it, then I was going to join you for a cuddle.'

'Oh, you can have the bed all to yourself, Mummy. I'm not sleepy at all.' He bounced up and down as though to prove his point.

'Terrific,' she murmured, smothering a yawn, and Trent chuckled.

'Is someone else sleeping in my bed?' Robby continued his inquisition.

'Yes. His name is Greg,' she informed him, knowing he would want to know everything. 'There are also two other men, one called Dan, one called Phil, who are in the spare room. Phil is very sick so I want you to keep out of there, all right?'

'Can I say hello, though?'

'Perhaps, but only if I'm with you.'

'What about Trent? Can I say hello if he's with me?'

'I guess so.'

'What about Aunty Maggie? Or Uncle Billy? If they're with me then can I say hello?'

'Yes,' she sighed, searching for patience. Dealing with Robbie and his non-stop chatter was tiring at the best of times, let alone when she was exhausted.

'But not on my own.'

'That's right.'

'What about Mr Rabbit?' He continued to bounce on the bed.

'No. Mr Rabbit is not a grown-up. He's your toy, remember.'

'But can I bring him when I go to say hello?'

'Robbie.' She stilled him. 'Enough. Go to the toilet and then come out to the lounge room. I need to look at Trent's scratches and bandage his leg.'

'OK.' He raced off to her *en suite,* his little feet pattering quietly on the cool floor.

'He's full of energy,' Trent murmured with a smile. 'Is he always so bright when he wakes up?'

'More so. The only problem is, after four and a half years I've yet to find the "off" switch.'

Trent chuckled and Aracely smothered another yawn. 'My body, however, has a definite "off" switch and I think it's been activated.'

'Look, don't worry about—'

'Stop it,' she said, and stood up, pushing renegade strands of hair back from her face. 'I'm looking at your injuries and that's all there is to it. Then I'm sleeping and Robby will just have to play quietly in here until my body is rested.'

'All right, then,' Trent said as Robby finished in the bathroom and raced out of his mother's bedroom. Trent followed the little boy, thinking that having Robby around might actually provide some distraction from the thought of Aracely touching him. He knew it was just first aid, he knew it needed to be done, but at the moment he was as intensely aware of her, of her presence, of her scent, which seemed to overpower him whenever he got too close to her, as he'd been just before Robby had called out. Yes, with Robby around, he wouldn't feel so self-conscious around Aracely.

She walked out to the lounge room and saw that he'd picked up the things she'd dropped earlier on and laid them out on the small table next to the sofa-bed. Robby had pulled back the covers on one side of the sofa-bed and climbed beneath them. 'Honey, no. That's where Trent's sleeping.'

'But, Mummy, my toes are cold,' he stated.

'It's all right,' Trent said, smiling at the little boy. 'Leave him where he is for now.'

Aracely shrugged and sorted out what she'd need first.

'Oh, Mummy. Look.' Robby was pointing at the bird's cage where the budgie had his head buried beneath his wing. 'You forgot to put the cover on the cage.'

'Who forgot?' she asked, picking up the cover. 'It's supposed to be your job to look after Charlie.'

'Oops,' he said, grinning from ear to ear and not looking the least bit sorry.

'Does it matter?' Trent asked, and Aracely laughed.

'If Charlie isn't covered, the instant he gets a glimpse of the sun, he starts squawking at the top of his little lungs. Not what we're after this morning.'

'Ah, so you're acknowledging it's morning now?' Trent teased, and she merely shrugged her shoulders.

'I'm past caring. Right. Let's get you sorted out.' She picked up the few bandages, sticking plasters and antiseptic she'd brought in earlier. 'The sooner we start, the sooner we finish, and we can both get some sleep.' She was careful not to say, 'and we can both go to bed', knowing full well she would have been embarrassed if he'd taken the double meaning. Clearing her throat, she worked hard at trying to exude profession-alism. 'Take off your shirt, please. Let me check your back first.'

Trent nodded and sat on the sofa-bed, turning his back to Aracely and talking quietly to Robby.

'Your mum tells me you're four and a half.'

Robby nodded proudly. 'I'm going to be five soon and then I get to go to school and Aunty Maggie's going to have a baby when I'm at school and when I get home from school every day I can go over and give it a bottle of milk. Aunty Maggie promised.'

'I'm sure she'll be glad of your help,' Trent agreed.

Robby settled back amongst the pillows, a soft toy cradled in his arms.

'And is this Mr Rabbit?' Trent asked, pointing to the toy.

'Yes. My mummy bought him for me when I was still in her tummy and it's my bestest toy ever.'

'He looks very…loved,' Trent said of the tatty toy.

Robby yawned, his words starting to slur a little. 'I have lots of toys and I love my trucks and I play with them every day, don't I, Mummy?'

'Yes, you do,' she murmured, glad Robby was here to diffuse the tension between herself and Trent. The fact that Trent was sitting in front of her, stripped to the waist, his bronzed skin glimmering enticingly in the firelight, was enough to send her pulses racing out of control. No, she needed to keep a level head and concentrate on her work rather than the giving in to the desire to run her fingers lightly over his skin, to lean forward and press kisses to his wounds in the hope it would make them all better.

He was a magnificent male specimen and where she'd known he was in good physical condition, *seeing* it was another matter altogether. The one thing that kept her mind focused was the actual damage to his skin. A large bruise across the back of his shoulders, which reached around to the front of his chest, was already starting to turn purple.

'What on earth did you do?' she asked rhetorically, frowning as she peered more closely at the cuts. Pulling on a pair of gloves, she reached for the disinfectant. While she worked, Trent continued to chat with Robby but when he was silent for over a minute, she glanced at her son to see his eyes closed, Mr Rabbit snuggled into his neck and his breathing deep and even.

'At least this means I'll be able to get some sleep,' she said quietly, but knew with Robby falling asleep, they'd lost their chaperon. 'I need to debride this one,' she said, reaching for a pair of scissors. 'Tell me if this hurts because I can put some topical anaesthetic gel around it.'

'It's fine,' he grunted, sucking in a breath as she snipped a small piece of dead skin away.

'Yeah, right. I don't really believe you.' She finished cleaning the area before sticking butterfly bandages over the cut to hold it closed so it could heal without the scar being too bad. 'I don't know if you realise how bad your back looks.' She peered at a gash around the left side of his body. 'I don't need to stitch any of them but you really took a beating out there. How have you been able to handle the fabric against your skin?'

'I'm a tough guy,' came his answer.

'Oh, sure. A tough guy. Women love tough guys like you,' she quipped. 'Turn around.'

Trent shifted away from her. 'It's all right. I can manage the ones in front.' But as he spoke, Aracely stood and came to sit on the other side of him. She shook her head in disgust when she saw the rope burn around the top of his waist. She pulled off her gloves and tentatively touched the burn. 'What on earth were you doing?' she exclaimed. 'No. Don't tell me. I don't want to know.' Her imagination could quite easily make a picture of the danger he'd put himself in.

Trent sucked in a sharp breath as her fingers made contact and he clenched his jaw, closing his eyes momentarily as he worked hard to ignore the effects of her touch on his body. Couldn't the woman see that she was driving him to distraction?

He was still trying to come to terms with the fact that he'd almost kissed Aracely earlier. That was so unlike him. Ever since he'd caught Tessa in bed with his cousin, he'd made it a point of order to steer clear of romantic entanglements, yet there was something about Aracely…something so intriguing, something… He couldn't put his finger on exactly what it was.

She appeared caring and genuine, relaxed and happy, and she was also sitting way too close, smelling sweet like a meadow filled with flowers on a beautiful spring day. He looked at her through hooded lids, noticing the hair he'd tucked behind her ear had worked itself loose again and was dangling down by her cheek. It was a perfect curl and he longed to wind it around his finger, to be able to touch those glorious dark locks of hers. He'd always been a sucker for women with long gorgeous hair and Aracely was proving to be no exception. And her eyes…they were deep brown and amazingly expressive.

He'd seen humour, annoyance, impatience and frustration, each one slightly different, but it was the way she'd looked at him earlier, when he'd been so hypnotised by her that his gut had twisted into knots. When he'd slowly made his way to stand in front of her, the desire, the need, the total longing he'd seen in the depths of her eyes had affected him as he'd never been affected before.

Staring into her face, he'd seen flecks of gold in her eyes and it had been that which had driven him to touch her, to give in to the urge to tuck her hair behind her ear, and he'd nearly ruptured with longing.

Even now, at the memory, he was having difficulty controlling the way she made him feel—or perhaps that was because she'd just finished rubbing some cream into his burn and was now cleaning the rest of his cuts and abrasions with the disinfectant. It was cruel. It was torture and although he was enraptured with every movement her long, lean fingers made, he knew he couldn't do anything about it. Although he was intrigued by her, captivated by her, she had her life and he had his. Trent looked across at her sleeping son and his gut twisted with repressed pain.

It was clear that Aracely adored her son and that was great to see, but at the same time it brought back so much of the pain he'd experi-

enced on learning the truth about the child his
wife had been carrying. She'd told him it was his,
that he was going to be a father. Trent had been
elated at the prospect. He'd also naïvely hoped
that their unborn child would unite them, might
help to fix the problems in their marriage…but
he'd been wrong.

The child hadn't been his after all. Instead, the
honour of fatherhood had gone to his cousin,
who'd been having an affair with Tessa. To say
he'd felt like a fool was an understatement.

Aracely dabbed some antiseptic to a particu-
larly deep cut and he winced in pain, bringing his
thoughts back to the present. He looked at her
once more and this time remembered the fear
and uncertainty he'd seen in her eyes when he'd
been so close to kissing her.

'Sorry,' she whispered, her breath fanning
across his skin.

Trent groaned, closing his eyes as the longing
he felt for her bubbled to the surface once more.

'Almost finished.'

He opened his eyes and their gazes met, and it
was then she saw that where she'd thought he'd

been moaning in pain, it was something quite different that was causing him distress.

'I can finish it off,' he said carefully.

'But I'm almost done,' she reiterated, but her hands were still, her eyes captured by his, the tension and awareness winding around them once more. Aracely swallowed and mentally gave herself the clinical spiel. She was a doctor. He was her patient. He needed her help.

'It's fine. Really.' Trent rose to his feet and moved away as though to prove his point. The problem was that he stood up so quickly he put too much pressure on his injured leg and almost tripped over the coffee-table. He straightened up and shifted his weight to his good leg. 'I can definitely handle the rest. Thanks, though. What you've already done is much appreciated.' He reached for his discarded shirt and put it on, gingerly pulling it over his head.

She pulled off her gloves and started tidying up, but Trent knew he couldn't watch her any more. He needed to do something—anything—except look at her. He crossed to the fire and stoked it.

'What about your leg?' she asked. 'Do you want me to look at that?'

Was she insane? Trent took three deep breaths, shutting the door to the slow combustion stove before slowly straightening and turning to face her. 'Leave me the anti-inflammatory gel and a bandage. I'll take care of it.'

Aracely nodded, leaving out the two items he'd requested. 'All right. I'll get an ice pack for you as well and hunt out some extra pillows for you to rest it on.'

'That would be great. Rest, ice, compression and elevation. Good ol' RICE. That's all it needs.'

'I also think you should take some ibuprofen.'

'OK.' Trent nodded, ready to agree to anything if it meant she'd leave him alone. He just needed a few minutes to get himself under control again and then everything would be back to normal, but even as the thought passed through his mind, he knew it wasn't the truth any more. Aracely Smith was affecting him more deeply than he'd realised and the urge to kiss her, which had just been a whim before, was now becoming a deep-seated desire and one that was only growing stronger every moment he spent in her presence. Once he was out of Port Wallaby, Aracely would stop causing him so much trouble. He'd be able to get back to his life—the well-ordered, well-structured life where he was in control and wasn't bothered by dark-haired beauties.

He tried not to watch her as she moved around the room, putting the medical supplies into the cupboard and the rubbish into the bin. 'I won't lock the cupboard in case you need anything during the night for yourself or one of your friends. Usually I keep it locked, in case there's a break-in or something.' He nodded, trying to concentrate on her words. Now that she'd finished ministering to him, the realisation of how she'd been touching his body, of running her fingers over his skin, was starting to sink in.

'Good thinking.'

Both were still and an uncomfortable silence settled over them until Aracely spoke, pointing to the hallway. 'I'll go get those things for you, then I'll come and move Robby.'

'Thanks.' Trent watched her go, relief washing over him. He closed his eyes and shook his head. Why had he even agreed to let her touch him? It was ridiculous and now he couldn't wait to leave.

The sooner he put half a country's worth of distance between himself and the gorgeous Dr Smith, the better he'd be. Never before had a woman been so able to frazzle his senses so easily.

He lay down on the sofa-bed, waiting for her to return with the ice pack and pillows. Until his head touched the pillow, he hadn't realised just how exhausted his body was. Adrenaline had spurred him on ever since the storm had first hit. That had been about twelve hours ago and now he was drained.

When Aracely came back into the room, it was to find Trent stretched out on the covers of the sofa-bed, his eyes closed. She put the glass of water and the other things she'd brought in down on the table before crossing to his side. 'Trent?' she called softly, but received no response. 'Trent?' This time, she was a little louder and put her hand on his right shoulder and gently shook. No response.

She pressed her fingers to his pulse and counted. He was fine. Exhaustion had claimed him and she decided against trying to wake him. His leg, however, needed to be treated. She arranged the extra pillows at the end of the sofa-bed, gathered the gel, bandage and ice pack and put them on the floor beside her.

Next, she took off his sock and rested his injured foot on the pillow. The elevation would give her access to his calf muscle and she pushed the fabric of his borrowed jeans up to his knee.

He had nice legs, she noted and glanced at his face, feeling guilty for ogling a sleeping man. His eyes were still closed, his breathing still even, and she returned her attention back to the task at hand. 'The sooner you start, the sooner you can finish,' she whispered quietly to herself, and, sitting on the edge of the bed, she picked up the gel and squeezed some onto her hands, trying to warm it a little before rubbing it into his skin. Her hands began to tingle both from the texture of his leg and also because of what she was doing. She was gently massaging a man's leg and not just any man, but one she found herself feeling dangerously attracted to.

'Be professional,' she lectured herself sternly, and once she'd finished she picked up the bandage and wound it around his leg. She was able to shift the fabric of his jeans back into place over the bandage and then put a small cushion beneath his leg for the ice pack to rest on.

He didn't wake during the entire procedure and she was relieved. She tidied up and went to wash her hands, knowing she had enough time to have a quick drink, brush her teeth and her hair, and check on her three other patients before heading back to Trent to remove the ice pack.

Greg, Dan and Phil were all sleeping. She changed Phil's saline bag as well as switching his catheter bag. Greg's temperature was still stable and Dan was sleeping peacefully. When she returned to Trent it was to find he hadn't moved but Robby had shifted, snuggling in closer to the warmth provided by Trent's body.

The two of them made a sight and it was one that turned her heart, making her realise there was indeed a hole in her life. She had coped with everything that had been thrown at her—an unhappy marriage, the discovery of her pregnancy, the accident, the destroyed surgical dreams, the pleasure of Robby's birth—everything. She'd coped and until this moment she'd thought she'd been doing all right, but she wasn't. Something was missing and it was having a man in her life. Not just any man either, but one who would be supportive, encouraging, have a strong sense of family, be a husband to her and a father to Robby. In short, a man like Trent.

She looked down at him, gazing at his strong face, now relaxed in sleep. Here was a man who really cared for his friends. Jaden, Robby's father, hadn't been like that at all. He was a career man, driven by dollars and cents rather than emotions. He hadn't seemed that way when they'd first met, when she'd married him after a whirlwind romance. He'd seemed to have direction and clear intent on what he wanted out of life. She'd found that very appealing back then, but when she'd seen that he lived every aspect of his life in that same little box, it had saddened her. That sadness had turned to desolation when Jaden, on learning of her pregnancy, had declared he'd never wanted to be a father, that it hadn't been in his plan and that she should 'take care of it'.

Aracely shook her head, clearing her thoughts. They didn't hurt her any more and she knew she'd had a lucky escape, but that didn't stop her from wanting a man in her life, a *true* man. Robby stirred and she realised she had to get moving or she'd still be standing there, watching Trent sleep, when the sun finally peeked over the horizon.

She was pleased, though, that she'd had the opportunity to study him without him knowing. The stress lines he'd had for most of the night had relaxed and she even noted a small scar at the bottom of his chin. Unable to curb the impulse, she reached out and gently ran her finger along it, wondering how he'd got it.

When his eyes snapped open and his hand shot up to capture her wrist, Aracely gasped in fright, the sudden pounding of her heart temporarily deafening her. He stared at her for a moment and she saw his expression change from trepidation to one of relaxed desire.

'It's you,' he murmured, his grip loosening a little on her arm…but he didn't let her go. Instead, his fingers slid from her wrist down to her hand, smoothing and caressing her in such a way that Aracely was unable to breathe for a moment.

He brushed his thumb across the backs of her knuckles before tugging her a little closer so he could put his lips in the exact same place. He breathed onto her skin in a deep and controlled way, as though he was trying with all his might to rein in the fire that was threatening to burn bright and fast.

For another moment she allowed him to continue before she found the strength and the power to jerk her hand free. 'Don't,' she whispered, the word barely audible. Quickly she went around to the other side of the sofa-bed and leaned down to gather Robby into her arms.

'Don't forget Mr Rabbit,' Trent said, holding the toy out to her.

She took it from him without a word and, with her son resting in her arms, thankfully still asleep, she hurried to the safety of her own room.

Never in her life or in her wildest dreams had a man ever touched her in such an overpowering and intimate manner. All he'd done had been to hold her hand and kiss it—that was all—yet the way he'd done it had been so…alluring. It was as though he had been promising her something special and the big problem with that was, Aracely knew she *wanted* it.

CHAPTER SEVEN

TRENT had always been one of those people to wake up in the morning and instantly know where they were and what was happening around them, so it came as a complete surprise to him when he woke up, sat bolt upright in bed and stared at his surroundings, not having the first clue where he was or why he was there.

The room was warm and he glanced at the slow combustion fire, surprised it hadn't burnt out. A bird was chirping brightly in its uncovered cage. As he shifted, he winced at the pain in his leg and then in a rush everything came flooding back. The fishing trip, the storm, the rescue—Aracely. He lay back amongst the pillows and thought. Aracely Smith. He'd been waiting for her last night, waiting for medical supplies. Had she come or had she fallen asleep and forgotten?

He felt his leg. It was bandaged but he couldn't remember doing it. All he could remember was dreaming about the woman who was responsible for his present hospitality. Dreaming? He frowned. He'd dreamt she'd been standing beside the bed, caressing his face, touching his scar. The frown grew deeper. Had it been a dream?

No. It had been real. He'd held her hand, had kissed it, and he'd been assailed by such a powerful need to be with her, he wasn't sure what to do about it now. Then she'd collected her son and disappeared to her room. Even as he remembered he once more felt that same desire—the one that said he'd be a fool to leave today, to not take the opportunity that had been handed to him…the opportunity to get to know Aracely Smith a lot better.

The phone rang and he heard footsteps heading up the hallway, then the phone stopped. Trent realised Aracely probably had clinic or house calls or perhaps the call was about transferring the four of them to Moonta or possibly to Adelaide. He looked out the window and could see daylight around the edges of the curtains.

The wind appeared to still be howling but he couldn't hear rain. He spotted a neat pile of what looked to be his clothes folded neatly on the dining-room table, his boots still by the fire where he'd put them last night. Good. At least he could change into his own clothes, which definitely fitted him better and were infinitely more comfortable. Then again, Aracely wouldn't be able to tease him about his trousers being too short and she probably wouldn't look at him the way he'd caught her staring last night when he'd been stretching. He groaned as he recalled how deep and dark her eyes had been, reflecting the confusion, the need and the desire that had been mixed up inside her.

He didn't want to cause confusion in her life and it was true that he hadn't been looking for anything like this…this thing that seemed to exist between them. However, it had happened. He was attracted to Aracely and if her reactions to his few brief touches were anything to go by, she was right there with him, fighting just as hard to ignore it.

But should he? He'd learnt in the past that

ignoring problems only gave them more power to blow up and spiral out of control. He'd known his marriage wasn't perfect, had suspected his wife might have been having an affair, but he hadn't wanted to admit it to himself. He'd ignored it and bad things had happened. If he ignored what he was feeling for Aracely, if he left Port Wallaby today, never to return, would it be something he would regret for the rest of his life?

Trent had this week and next week off as annual leave so he had no patients or operating lists that were urgent to get back to. He'd planned to spend some time fishing with his buddies and then sorting through his books back at his apartment and alphabetising them, something he'd been meaning to do ever since Tessa had moved out.

It sounded dull and boring even to him, especially when compared with the alternative. Staying here in Port Wallaby would be a change of pace, a change of style, and it would also give him pleasure to help Aracely, especially during the next few days with the extra damage and medical cases the storm brought with it.

He heard the phone ring again and realised it

was time he stopped lying around thinking about things and started putting his thoughts into action. Ten minutes later Aracely came into the lounge room carrying a backpack and picked up a set of keys off the chair-side table, stuffing them into her jeans pocket. She was dressed in a rust-coloured turtle-neck jumper, which fitted her glorious shape to perfection. Sturdy boots and black denim made her look warm and cosy. Trent filled his lungs at the sight of her and slowly exhaled, the mild scent of her perfume tantalising him once again. He liked it.

'Good morning,' Trent said as he finished packing the sofa-bed away.

'Yes. It's definitely morning now.'

His smile was instant. 'You managed to sleep?'

'Yes, thank goodness.'

'And Robby?'

'He allowed me to sleep until eight-thirty, which I thought was very generous of him.'

'Was he quiet? I mean, I didn't hear him.'

Aracely shrugged. 'He played with his toys, read books. I guess I'm used to snoozing with him chattering in the background. He's usually pretty good at entertaining himself.' Aracely paused and briefly allowed herself to take in his attire. Man, he looked good. 'H-how are you feeling?' She cleared her throat, surprised at her stutter.

He twisted his body from side to side and winced. 'Every muscle seems to be aching.'

'That's a very natural reaction. And your leg?'

'It's fine. Er…thank you for bandaging it last night.'

'No problem.' She shrugged and walked to the medical cupboard, opening it and peering inside. 'Greg's awake and feeling much better,' she reported. 'Dan is in talking to Greg and Phil is dozing happily, pain medication still doing the trick. I've changed his saline and catheter bags so he should be fine while I'm gone.'

'Where are you going?' He sat on the sofa and started pulling on his boots.

'House calls.'

'Where's Robby?'

'Preschool. Storm or no storm, it's a typical Wednesday morning and I have more people than normal who want my attention.' She smothered a yawn.

'And you're running on empty.'

'Oh, no. Maggie's already been over and plied me with very strong coffee, toast and home-made jams.'

'Sounds delicious. I gather she brought my clothes as well.'

'Yes. The bread's in the kitchen and I think there's still some coffee left in the pot so help yourself.' She finished packing her bag and locked the cupboard.

'How about I help you instead?'

Aracely stopped, startled. 'Sorry?'

'I can help you. With your house calls,' he added when she looked at him as though he was speaking another language.

'Oh, it's all right. I should be fine. Maggie's going to pick Robby up from preschool and although I have a full list of people to see, it shouldn't be too draining.'

'Seriously, Aracely. I'm happy to help. Don't tell me you're one of those people who don't accept help when they know they really need it?'

'Aren't you?'

'Yes, but that's not what we're talking about.

I'm here, I'm more than qualified and I can't recall ever having done a house call in my life. All my patients come to see me at the hospital so you see it'll be something of a novelty.'

'A novelty, eh?' Her lips twitched as she thought. She would have people turning up here at the clinic this afternoon and if she didn't get going and get the house calls done, she'd be running late all day long. 'I do have a lot to do,' she said out loud. 'And you can't leave until Billy gives the OK that the creek's receded enough to use the boat to transfer you and your friends.'

'So I can go with you?' Trent was surprised at how excited he was at the prospect.

'How about we start you off slow? I'll get these house calls done and you take care of anyone who turns up for the clinic scheduled for this afternoon. It's a first come, first seen basis—unless a particular case is an emergency, of course.'

'Of course.' He tried to hide his disappointment at not being able to spend more time with her but he'd offered help and he would do what she needed.

'OK, then. That's settled.' The phone rang

again and she groaned. 'If only I had a life,' she muttered as she headed off to answer it.

Trent stood at the kitchen window and watched as she reversed out of her driveway and headed off for her house calls. He turned and leaned against the bench, sipping his coffee. Life seemed different here and it intrigued him. The pace, though perhaps a little accelerated today due to last night's events, was slower than in Sydney. It was…comfortable. Until that moment, he hadn't realised just how dissatisfied he was with his life. His well-ordered, structured life. The life he'd dug himself into after Tessa had left. Routine was what had got him through those first few months as he'd dealt with the failure of his marriage, her rejection of him as a man and not being the father of the baby. Work had been his saving grace but now he slowly realised all he'd been doing had been existing.

Last night, with the storm, he'd felt alive and this morning that feeling was still there. Was it because he'd risked life and limb last night? Or was it because Aracely responded to him—

not as a doctor but as a woman who was interested in a man.

She'd given him a brief run-down on where to find things before she'd left, and he'd watched her with a half-smile as she'd flitted about her consulting room, pointing things out, but it was when she'd been at the door, backpack on her shoulder, keys in her hand, about to leave, that something had flipped in his stomach.

'Thanks for this,' she'd said, her words filled with gratitude.

'Happy to help,' he'd responded, and then it had happened again. That sense, that growing need that existed between them. It was as though an invisible bond was forming between them, like a huge piece of elastic, drawing them closer, into each other's lives, before snapping them back, putting distance between them.

Trent exhaled slowly, recalling the way her lips had parted, her eyes had darkened and she'd pushed a stray curl out of her face with a trembling hand. He was positive that had he given in to the urge to close the distance between them, to take her in his arms and press his mouth to hers, she wouldn't have objected.

Instead, they'd both stood their ground before the phone had rung once again, breaking the moment. She'd closed her eyes for a second, as though totally hating the inanimate object, then she'd turned and walked away, leaving him stunned.

He drained his cup. Aracely was attracted to him and that in itself bolstered his spirits. She'd been hurt before, both of them had been through bad marriages, but somehow she gave him a sense of hope and it wasn't one he was going to brush aside.

The laughter that came from one of the bedrooms broke through his thoughts and he headed off to see his friends.

When Aracely eventually arrived home, it was much much later than she'd anticipated. The sun was already starting to set and she felt a sadness in her heart that she'd been unable to say goodbye to Trent. It was silly because she hardly knew the man. They were just doctors who had passed like ships in the night. She smiled to herself at the analogy.

Billy had called her a few hours ago to say he was ready to transfer them, but as she'd been unable to leave the patient she'd been with, she'd miss being there. Heaving her backpack from the car, she walked up the path that separated her place from Maggie's, looking forward to seeing her son. Whenever she had a bad day, Robby was always the light of her life, his constant smiles and laughter enough to lift her spirits and let her see the rainbow that surrounded her once more.

She knocked on the door to her sister's house before going in. 'Just me,' she called, and was surprised to find her brother-in-law sitting in his favourite chair, watching television.

'Hey, Cely.'

'Hi. Where's Robby?'

'At your house. Mags is over there, putting your dinner in the oven.'

'Oh. OK. So the transfer went all right?'

'Everything went smoothly. I think Phil was in quite a bit of pain when we transferred him across in the boat, but Trent gave him something for the pain. Last I knew they were safe and sound in Moonta hospital, being treated like visiting medical royalty, and they're due to fly out to Adelaide, then Sydney tomorrow.'

Aracely nodded, her throat too dry to speak. Trent had gone. Gone with his friends, gone back to his life in Sydney. It was what was supposed to happen, the way things were supposed to pan out, yet she still couldn't shake the desolate feeling that continued to swamp her. Why should she be so upset that Trent had left? She could always call him at Moonta hospital tonight, just check with him that everything had gone well and apologise that she hadn't been able to make it. Yes, that's what she'd do, she thought as she said goodnight to Billy and headed back to her house. She shook her head as she stepped through her back door, amazed that even the thought of speaking to Trent on the phone had her stomach fluttering in excitement.

'Hello?' she called, expecting Robby to come hurtling down the hallway towards her like he usually did. He didn't come. Aracely left her backpack on her consulting-room desk, noticing that nothing was out of place. Hmm, perhaps Trent hadn't had any patients turn up or maybe they'd turned up after he'd left. She hadn't received any calls on her mobile so it was obvious nothing urgent had happened which had required her attention.

Aracely continued through the house, heading towards the kitchen, when she heard Robby squeal. She quickened her pace and rushed into the living room to find her son jumping up and down, laughing with glee.

She smiled, instant relief that he was all right flooding through her. 'What are you—?' She stopped, stunned, when Trent stood up. He'd been lying on the floor, obscured from her vision by the sofa. 'Trent!'

'Hi, there. How were house calls?'

'What are you doing here?' Her tone was filled with incredulity.

'Playing with Robby,' he stated, and smiled at her son.

'I can see that but I thought you were…going. That you'd gone. Moonta. Adelaide. Sydney. With your friends.'

'I know what you mean, Aracely.'

'Do it again, Trent. Do it again,' Robby begged,

jumping up and down and tugging on Trent's hand. 'Watch, Mummy. Watch me. I'm gonna fly. Come on Trent. Do it again.'

Trent shrugged and knelt down on the carpet before lying on his back and taking Robby's hands in his. 'Ready?' he asked.

'Watch me, Mummy.' Robby squealed with delight again as Trent put his feet on Robby's waist and lifted him high in the air like an aeroplane. 'I'm flying.' With complete balance and total trust, Robby let go of Trent's hands and flung them out to the side, making aeroplane noises. Aracely was amazed at the delight on her son's face and then her heart jumped into her throat when Trent tossed Robby in the air with his feet, then quickly sat up to catch him.

Her jaw fell open as Robby wound his arms around Trent's neck, giggling with unabandoned happiness. Never before had she seen her son take to someone so readily, so completely, and she felt a twisting in her stomach at seeing man and boy together. It rammed home to her yet again that Robby didn't have a father, no one to toss him around, play with him as Trent was doing now.

Robby was laughing so hard and wriggling from side to side that she thought he was going to choke, but a moment later he was up on his feet, running towards her. 'See, Mummy. Did you see me flying? I was flying. I love flying.' He clung to her legs as he spoke then raced back to Trent, still giggling. 'Do it again, Trent. I want to do it again.'

'I want you to go to the toilet,' Aracely stated, and received a cross look from her son. 'Go on. Hurry up.' Robby hesitated for a moment, saw the determined look in his mother's eyes and decided to follow instructions, racing past her and down to the bathroom, almost knocking Maggie over in his haste.

'Whoa. Cyclone Robby strikes again.' Maggie chuckled. 'Your dinner is in the oven, heating up,' she announced.

'Thanks, Mags.' Aracely crossed to her sister's side and put her hand on her forehead. 'You feeling all right?'

'I'm fine. Just a little tired, although I feel as though I've slept most of the day away.'

'I'm sure you haven't,' Aracely returned. 'Go home and put your feet up. Doctor's orders.'

'Yes, my bossy sister,' Maggie said meekly, and bade both of them goodnight, stopping in the bathroom on the way to say goodnight to Robby.

'See? Even your own sister thinks you're bossy,' Trent said as he walked towards her.

'Hmm. Bossy or not, what are you doing here?'

'You said I could stay.'

'When?'

'This morning.'

'I never said that.'

'Sure you did. I offered to help and you said I could start with the clinic.'

'That's right, but nowhere do I recall asking you to give up your time to stay in Port Wallaby.'

'You don't need to ask me to give up my time. I'm more than willing to offer it.'

'But you have patients, clinics back in Sydney. People will have been on waiting lists for months and months just to get an appointment with you, let alone an operation. It's hardly professional just to call and say you're not coming back for a while.'

'You're right. That would be highly unprofessional. Luckily for me, I'm not unprofessional. I'm on annual leave and was supposed to be enjoying a relaxing fishing trip with my friends, but that plan's gone to pot.'

'So instead you're going to stick around here and help me out?'

'And give Robby aeroplane rides,' he added.

'Yes, and what about that? You have an injured leg, Dr Mornington, or have you conveniently forgotten?'

'It's much better today,' he said, smiling at her and waggling his eyebrows up and down. 'Must have been your Florence Nightingale touch last night when you bandaged my muscle.'

Aracely frowned at his teasing words. 'I'm a doctor, not a nurse.'

'Whatever. Look, you need help, I'm happy to stay and provide it. Besides, you promised I could do house calls with you.'

'I never promised anything of the sort,' she said, but could feel herself capitulating. Trent hadn't left. He was still there and she was secretly delighted about it. She tilted her head to the side, curls cascading over her shoulder. 'Do you always twist other people's words to suit your own purpose?'

He thought about that for a moment and she could already see the teasing light in his eyes which made her pulse rate quicken. Did the man have any idea just how irresistible he was? 'Not always,' he eventually confessed. 'Only when I want something really, really bad.'

'You want to stay in Port Wallaby that much?'

'I want to stay here and help *you* that much,' he clarified, his words softer than before.

'Oh.' Where the atmosphere between them had been playful and jovial, it suddenly changed to one of intense need. 'Why?' The word was whispered through very dry lips as her heart rate continued to rise. He simply stood there, watching her, and for a moment she wondered whether he was going to answer at all.

'Well…' he finally began, 'apart from the fact that due to last night's storm you need a bit of extra help, I…well…I want to help. I'm more than capable, I have annual leave I've been forced to take, so…' He shrugged. 'Why not?'

His words were logical, carefully thought out and it simply showed Aracely he wasn't a highly impulsive man. 'You're someone who thinks through all the angles, aren't you,' she stated, still trying to grasp the fact that he wanted to be there. He nodded at her words. 'I'm not sure that's what you were doing last night but as there were extenuating circumstances—i.e. your friends' lives at stake—I'm willing to discount that. However, there's got to be more to it than you just wanting to stay and help, Trent.' Even as she spoke, she found it increasingly difficult to control the pounding of her erratic pulse, her mouth going dry as she finished speaking.

'Meaning?' he asked, taking a small step towards her.

Aracely forced herself to square her shoulders and remain in control. It was difficult when he was so near and getting nearer. She stood her ground both mentally and figuratively, needing to know exactly what Trent had in mind.

'Meaning if you're staying here to…well, because of what's…because of what seems to exist between us at the moment, I don't think that's a valid reason for you staying at all.'

'Why not?' He was almost standing toe to toe with her now and she raised her chin, unable to break the bond flowing between them. 'I don't know what this is, Cely,' he whispered, and she gasped as he used her nickname. 'I don't have the faintest idea what exists between us. I only know it's something I've never felt before. It's rare, it's unique and I won't lie to you, it did factor heavily in my decision to stay and help.'

He placed his hand on her shoulder, his deep words vibrating right through her being. 'I can't seem to get you off my mind. From the moment we met, I've been impressed by you. As a doctor, as a mother, as a woman.' The last three words were said with such heartfelt desire, she began to tremble.

'Trent.' Slowly she shook her head. 'We'd be mad.'

'Mad to ignore it or mad to follow it?'

'I don't know. Look, we don't really know the first thing about each other…'

'Which is another reason why I thought it might be good to stay.'

'So we can…?'

'Get to know each other, yes.' He gently brushed a loose curl behind her ears. 'Your hair is glorious,' he murmured, as though he was unable to contain himself any longer. His hand slid around the back of her neck and unclipped her hair, the dark strands bouncing loose of their bonds.

'Cely,' he whispered, and brought both hands into her hair, tilting her head upwards so her lips would be ready to meet his.

It was an agonising wait and time definitely seemed to have stopped but she didn't dare move in case she broke this moment, this intense moment which she seemed to have been waiting for ever. Her lips parted to let the pent-up air escape and Trent took advantage of that, finally brushing his lips feather-light over hers.

'Mummy!' came Robby's wail from the toilet. 'Mummy, come here. I need you to help me!'

Amazed and embarrassed laughter bubbled up and overflowed between them and Aracely collapsed into Trent's arms, her breathing wild yet somehow returning to normal as she rested her head momentarily on his chest.

'I'm sorry,' she said as she pulled back.

'Such a perfect moment.' Trent's eyes were twinkling. 'Go. Do the mummy thing.'

'Well, you said you wanted to help?' she offered, reluctantly moving away from him with a sigh of regret.

'*Medical* help, Aracely.' He chuckled.

'Oh. Now you're going to put conditions on it, eh?'

'Mummy!' Robby wailed insistently, and on a surprising light-hearted laugh Aracely turned and headed off to deal with her impatient son, unable to shake the delight running through her that Trent was there.

CHAPTER EIGHT

THE following day, Aracely was constantly amazed at how well Trent seemed to slip into her life. He ate an early breakfast with them, tying Robby's shoelaces while she packed his lunch. He started the clinic while Aracely took Robby to preschool and did a few quick house calls.

Thankfully the creek had now receded enough to let four-wheel-drive vehicles through, which meant the district nurse could help pick up the slack where some of her patients were concerned, especially those such as Winston Chapman, who needed dressings changed. One of her favourite patients, though, was her Uncle Robert, and she'd missed seeing him yesterday.

By the time she was ready to see her favourite uncle, Robby's morning session of preschool had finished so she collected her son and drove to Robert's house.

'Uncle Robby,' Robby yelled loudly with laughter as he rushed through the house and into his great-great-great uncle's open arms. The ninety-four-year-old man sat there waiting but scooped the boy up with utter delight.

'Ah, here's me little mate.' Uncle Robert tickled the boy's tummy and then affectionately rubbed his head. 'I've got a surprise for you.'

'It's another truck. It's another truck.' Robby jumped around like a jelly bean.

'No foolin' you, is there, matey?' Uncle Robert produced the toy and Robby instantly dropped to the floor, playing with it and making truck noises.

'You spoil him,' Aracely commented.

'And who else am I gonna spoil, eh? Not many people get to see the likes of four generations after them,' Uncle Robert said, turning his attention to his great-great-niece.

'Oh, so I actually get some attention, do I?' Aracely joked, but she had to admit she loved watching the two Roberts together. One so old, one so young, yet somehow they were both the same. She kissed his cheek.

'Everything sorted out from the rescue the other night? Town's still reeling but it isn't the worst storm which has swept through here.'

'Thank goodness for that.' She went through the little kitchen, filled the kettle and switched it on before getting the cups out.

'Mags called me last night,' Robert called. 'Told me about the handsome doctor who seems to have caught your eye.' Uncle Robert had been a part of this community all his life. He was known and respected by everyone and his favourite pastime was taking great delight in teasing his great-great-nieces whenever he got the chance. Today appeared to be no exception.

'Oh, stop,' she said, coming back into the living room. 'He's just helping me out while he's on annual leave.'

'Good, cause you need some help with all the running around you do.'

'Hmm, could that have anything to do with some of my patients who refuse to let the district nurse treat them?'

Uncle Robert frowned. 'I just don't trust her. That's all.'

'Just as well I'm used to your cantankerous ways.'

'Cantanker—You watch it, girlie,' he said with mock sternness. 'I'm not so old that I can't put you over my knee.'

'Yes, you are.' She laughed. The kettle switched itself off and she went to make the tea, bringing it in on a tray.

'So tell me about this young doctor,' Robert said as he accepted a steaming cup. 'Nice man? Stable? Think you can get him to move here?'

'Uncle Robert!' Aracely shook her head.

'What? I'm a man who doesn't have a lot of time and I need to know you'll be taken care of.'

'By a man I've only just met and know next to nothing about?'

'There's more to it than that,' he stated. 'I can see it in your face. You like him. Yep, I can tell. You have a certain…glow about you. As though you've just discovered a great big secret. I can already tell the man's made an impression on you.'

Aracely gazed at her uncle for a moment,

then shook her head. 'He won't be here for long and, yes, I like him but there's more to a relationship than just *like*. Besides, I have Robby to think about.'

'Yes, you do, and the boy's going to need more of a father figure than young Billy or ya dad can provide.'

'We've got you, too.'

He waved her words impatiently away. 'Listen, liking a boy is not such a bad place to start, Cely.' He chuckled. 'I was lucky to be blessed twice in love. Two wives I've had and outlived them both so I know what I'm talking about. That stupid boy who you married, thinking you loved him, was never the right one for you. He didn't care about you. He didn't care about Robby. He left you in the middle of your recovery and let me tell you, girlie, that if someone really cares for you, they stick around for the long haul. Through good and bad. Nah, he was no good for my Cely.'

'And you think Trent is, even though you've never met him.'

'Seeing this new light in your eyes is enough for me to think well of him already.'

'Hmm,' she mused again. 'I think we should get on with your medical check-up so I can get on with the rest of my day.'

'Stop changing the subject.'

'Have you been taking your tablets?'

'I'm too old to take tablets,' he protested. He was living in a retirement village but was one of the residents who was still able to care for himself which, given his age, was wonderful. Aracely was determined to keep him where he was for as long as he could manage, but if he started to refuse to take his meds, she wasn't sure that would be possible. 'I just don't want to.'

'Why not?'

'Because I want to die. It's my time.'

'Don't talk like that. You know it upsets me and, besides, who's going to tease me and tell me how to run my life if you're not here?'

Uncle Robert laughed. 'There'll be plenty of takers in this town, Cely.'

She pulled out her sphygmomanometer and took his blood pressure, shaking her head at the result. 'Uncle Robert, your blood pressure is up way too high. You need these tablets to control it.'

'I don't want to feel better.'

'The staff at the retirement village reported you've been having some trouble doing simple, everyday things. When did this start?'

'Nosy little things those girlies are,' he protested, and Aracely found it difficult to smother her smile.

'It's their job, Uncle Robert.' She grabbed the bottle of tablets she'd left him and took one out. 'Swallow it,' she ordered, and he harrumphed at that. 'I'm not leaving until I've seen you swallow your medication and don't try hiding it under your tongue or down the side of your teeth or even under your dentures. I know all the tricks in the book and you'll be swallowing that tablet whether you like it or not.'

'All right,' he grumbled, recognising a stalemate. 'I'm not a child so don't treat me like one.'

'Then stop acting like one,' she countered, and received a smile from him.

'You're bossier than the staff here.'

'That's my job.'

'Ha, the bossiness has got nothing to do with your job. You're just like your great-grandmother—my sister. You look like her, you talk like her, you were even named for her. It's uncanny,' he said, shaking his head.

Aracely smiled as she got him a glass of water. 'You say that every time I come.'

'That's because it's true.'

She handed him the tablet. 'Please, swallow this. For me,' she said softly, and he nodded. When it was down she quickly wrote in his notes before putting the file into her backpack and picking up her keys.

'So what's the verdict, Cely? You gonna let me die in peace or are you and the staff here going to bug me until me last breath?'

Aracely tilted her head to the side and thought about it for a moment. 'Bug you until your last breath,' she said, then smiled at him. 'Maggie and I need you far too much, not to mention Robby. Now, I'm going to give you one more chance to follow my instructions. If you stop taking your medication, I'll have to get the sister from the office to come over and administer it.'

'Oh, you play dirty, Cely. You play dirty.'

Aracely kissed his cheek and grinned. 'You

taught me everything I know, Uncle Robert.' She looked at her son. 'Time to go, darling.'

Robby was still in his own little world but after a minute or two he got up and at his mother's insistence, thanked Uncle Robert for his new truck then ran out to the car.

Uncle Robert followed her out and held the car door for her as she got in. 'I'll see you soon,' she promised him.

'You'd better, and next time you come, bring that new young doctor with you. I want the chance to check him out for myself. If he passes my inspection, you'll have my blessing.'

'I can't wait,' she drawled, before reversing out of his driveway. When she arrived home, she enjoyed lunch with Robby but there was no sign of Trent. She checked the consulting rooms but he wasn't about. Her first thought was that he'd changed his mind, that he'd decided to leave after all, but when she checked the spare room it was to find a duffle bag, which had seen better days, with the name MORNINGTON written on the tag around the handle.

'Still here, I see,' she murmured.

Her patients started arriving for afternoon clinic and with Robby settled in his bedroom, playing with his toys, she started work. After half an hour of consulting, she came out to find Trent calling a patient through and he smiled brightly at her, helping to alleviate the feeling that there was nothing wrong.

With Trent's help they got through plenty of patients and the day flew past. After dinner that evening, once she had Robby settled, which took a while after Trent had razzled him up again, she sat down at the dining-room table to get through her paperwork and referral letters.

'Did you say that you were looking for another GP?' Trent asked, pulling out a chair opposite her.

'The Peninsula Medical Service is, yes.'

'What about an orthopaedic surgeon?'

Aracely's eyebrows hit her hairline. 'What? Are you insane?'

'Why would I be insane?'

'You're thinking of moving here?'

'I'm merely asking questions, Aracely,' he returned with a smile.

She took a breath, calming herself down, trying

not to let her thoughts run ahead of themselves. 'We do currently have an orthopaedic surgeon who consults at Moonta hospital one day per month. He holds a clinic for three hours in the morning and then operates for another three hours in the afternoon.'

'That wouldn't really do much to diminish waiting lists.'

'It doesn't but we take what we can get. I usually do the anaesthetics for the ortho surgeon and sometimes the general surgeon.'

'Who I take it is also here on a monthly basis?'

'That's right.'

'But you're specifically looking for a GP to help out here?'

'Yes. There are other GPs in Moonta and, let's face it, Moonta isn't that far from here, but the population of Port Wallaby is also quite elderly and even fifteen to twenty minutes' travelling may not be good for their health. Since I took over the practice here, my patient lists have exploded, but I can't extend my consulting hours any more because of Robby. It's simply not fair to him.'

'So another GP here should do the trick to lighten the load?'

'Yes. Just two or three days a week. I doubt the area would support two full-time GPs but definitely a doctor who's willing to work part time.'

Trent nodded. 'Yet getting doctors to move from the city is a plight our government struggles with all over the country.'

'Exactly. Rural GPs are hard to come by and when you do find them they're overworked and underpaid, rarely getting the opportunity to take a holiday because it's even difficult to get locums to come out. As I said, I'm not so bad here.'

'You can take a holiday?'

'Yes. The Peninsula Medical Services shuffle us around and we pick up the slack so if one of the GPs in Moonta or Maitland takes leave, I'll go and consult there for two days a week.'

'And Robby?'

'Maggie has him. It's not all the time so it's all right and, besides, helping others means I get to take time off and take my son on holidays.'

He nodded, his expression pensive. 'Sounds like a good arrangement.'

'It is. Do you mind if I check over the files of the patients you've seen so far? Just so I know what's going on,' she added, when he raised his eyebrows.

'Sure.' He disappeared down to the rear of the house and returned with a stack of files. 'I thought as much, which is why I didn't re-file them.'

'It's not that I don't trust you.' The words came out in a rush, lest he should take offence.

'I know. You can't let go. They're your patients. You've been seeing them all for years. So what will happen, I wonder, if you do manage to get another doctor here? Will you check their work once the day is done or will you let them simply do their job?'

Aracely sighed. 'I guess I am a bit of a control freak.'

'No.' Trent shook his head. 'I wouldn't say that. I'd guess that you've had to be in tight control over the past few years but I'll let you in on a little secret—in fact, it's some excellent advice I was given not that long ago.' He leaned forward, putting both hands on the table and bringing his face close to hers. 'Find people you can trust and lean on them—professionally speaking, of course. Don't hold too tightly to those reins, Cely.' As he whispered the words, he realised they also applied to his own working life. 'I'm just as guilty as you,' he continued, his voice low, his words washing over her like soft silk. 'I've wrapped myself up in work for so long, even more so since my wife left me, that I fear taking a step out of it. Well, I *did* fear,' he clarified, slowly straightening up again. 'Now…I've realised it's not so bad.'

Aracely's brain was sluggish due to his nearness but she finally processed what he'd just said. 'That's why you stayed?'

'One of the reasons, yes. I was forced to take leave and if I hadn't come here, if I hadn't been out in that storm, if I hadn't met you…' He breathed in deeply. 'I might not have had the strength to take the step I'm now taking. For the first time in…' He shrugged. 'I can't remember how long, I don't know what's going to happen next.'

'With what?' she asked softly.

'With helping you out. With staying in your house. With meeting new people—*really* meeting them, not just having them as my patients who come and go day in, day out.' Trent shoved his hands into the pockets of his jeans. 'But most of all, I don't know what's going to happen with this thing between us.' A sexy smile twitched at his lips, his eyes deep and filled with promise.

How Aracely slept that night, she had no idea. What she *did* know was that her first thought was of Trent. The need to have his mouth pressed to hers once more and not just in a brief, butterfly kiss but one where she could really let her pent-up desire for him take its natural course was becoming more insistent.

'It's ridiculous,' she told her reflection as she dressed. 'He's just here to help you out.' She groaned and closed her eyes for a moment. Who was she kidding? She liked what she saw of him and she wanted more. More of the talking, of the discovery, of the way he thought. Being held in his arms, having his body close to hers and his mouth where she knew he would create absolute havoc with her senses.

No man, not even Jaden, had affected her in

such a way. With Jaden, it had been slow and steady. First they'd met as colleagues, then become friends, then when he'd weighed the pros and cons of having her in his life, he'd proposed. She'd been too naïve to realise Jaden never did anything that wasn't meticulously planned out.

Robby came into her room, breaking her thoughts and forcing her back to the present. 'Trent's made pancakes for breakfast,' he declared, and although there was a big grin on his face, he shook his head. 'Aunty Maggie isn't going to like that.'

Aracely followed her son and, sure enough, there was Trent in her tiny kitchen, a pink frilly apron around his waist, standing at the stove, flipping pancakes.

'I've been told Aunty Maggie disapproves of pancakes.'

'For breakfast,' Aracely said. 'As a dessert, however, she's fine with it.'

'What do you say?' he asked, raising his eyebrows.

'I say…it's Friday! Let's go for it.'

'Yay!' Robby clapped his hands then ran and wrapped his arms about Trent's leg. 'I love pancakes for breakfast.'

'So do I,' Trent remarked, and Aracely watched as wistfulness crossed his face as he ruffled Robby's hair.

'Uncle Robby does that to me,' Robby said as he pulled away, literally launching himself at his mother who bent to scoop him up.

'Who's Uncle Robby?' Trent asked, flipping the last pancake over.

'He's really old,' Robby informed him as Aracely cuddled and kissed her son before he squirmed in her arms and wriggled back down to the floor. 'He's almost a hundred!' The little boy's eyes bulged out of his head at the words.

'Really?' Trent raised an eyebrow as he carried the food to the table, which Aracely was surprised to find already set.

'He's not exaggerating,' Aracely said, and filled him in about Uncle Robert.

'He wants to meet you,' Robby added, waiting impatiently for his mother to cut up his food. 'He told Mummy to bring you over the next time we came.' Robby paused. 'He *did* mean Trent, right?'

'Yes, darling.'

'So I've been talked about, eh?' Trent seemed inordinately pleased.

'Probably by most of the town,' she replied. 'Mmm, these are delicious. What else can you cook?'

Trent smiled. 'Thinking of taking the pressure off Maggie while I'm here?'

Aracely nodded. 'Maggie needs to rest more, keep her feet up, but I think she's scared Robby and I will exist solely on pre-packaged foods.'

'Would you?'

'Probably.' Aracely sneezed and then shook her head. 'Where did that come from?'

'Are you 'lergic to pancakes, Mummy?' Robby wanted to know.

'Allergic,' she automatically corrected. 'And no. I don't think I've heard of a case where people have been allergic to pancakes.'

'Especially home-made ones, not pre-packaged,' Trent added with a gleam in his eyes.

'True.'

'So, the agenda for today?' Trent asked. 'What time do you have preschool, Master Robby?'

'I'm not a Master. I'm a Super-hero,' he stated, as though Trent was a complete ninny not to know that.

'No preschool on Fridays,' Aracely said. 'Usually we have the morning to ourselves but instead today we have a few more house calls to do as I'm still playing catch-up.'

'And what about you, Super-hero Robby? Do you go with Mummy on her house calls?'

'Nah. I wanna spend time with you, Trent,' he stated, his eyes lighting up.

'Ah. Well, actually, I was going to go with Mummy to see the sick people.'

Robby pondered this for a moment, his face falling at the news, but he brightened up immediately. 'I'll play with Uncle Billy, then. He's good at playing trucks. Can I take my new one?'

'Of course.'

'Yay.' He shovelled the last few mouthfuls of food into his mouth, then clambered down from the table.

'Wash your hands,' she called after him.

'Where's he going?'

'To get his new truck ready and pack his toys into his bag.'

Trent nodded. 'You read him very well.'

'He's my son.' Aracely's smile was bright and natural. 'When he was a baby, I could tell exactly what he needed by the way he cried.' She shrugged. 'All mothers can. Besides, with babies, it's usually one of five things. They either need changing, feeding, or burping. If it's none of those, they need a sleep or they need to play. That's it.'

'You make it sound so simple.' His tone was quiet and she caught the edge to his words. Now, mixed with the wistfulness came the look of regret and Aracely couldn't help but wonder just what had happened to him to put that look there.

'Want to talk about it?' she asked just as quietly.

At her words he seemed to snap out of wherever he'd just been and instantly covered his emotions over with a half-hearted smile. 'I'm fine.'

'You say that a lot, when you're really not.'

'If you're talking of my physical injuries, my scratches and gashes are healing well, my leg is feeling much better again today and I'm raring to go on my house-call expedition.'

Now she laughed, pleased that the smile was now touching his eyes. 'Well, OK, then. Let's get going.' She finished eating and gathered up the plates, carrying them to the kitchen. 'I just need to get things ready.'

'Then I'll take care of the dishes,' he offered, coming into the kitchen behind her.

It was such a small space. Such a small confined space. He was close, so close his scent encompassed her and she realised he was fresh from a shower. She wanted to move, to put some distance between them, but if she were to move back, she'd crash into him. If she moved to the side, she'd be stuck in the corner of the kitchen, which would be a worse scenario.

Aracely closed her eyes, wishing he'd give her some space, that he didn't affect her so completely just by having his body in close proximity to her own. She opened her eyes, realising he hadn't moved and she was now starting to feel the warmth of his body surrounding her back. She gripped the kitchen bench tighter, her knuckles going white while she worked hard at controlling her breathing.

'We keep meeting like this,' he murmured, his breath close to her ear. In the next instant he brushed her hair aside and pressed small kisses to her neck. 'I'm drawn to you, Cely. I can't help it.'

CHAPTER NINE

Tingles flooded her body, goose-bumps rose on her skin, making her tremble. His hands were on her shoulders and slowly he was turning her to face him.

'We can't,' she whispered as his mouth hovered dangerously close to hers. 'Robby.' She lifted a hand to rest on his chest, not to push him away but to let him know she felt exactly what he did.

Trent stole a quick kiss, then nodded, knowing they needed to be careful. 'You're right. I know but it's this…' He paused. 'Your skin is so soft.' He allowed himself the thrill of touching her cheeks as he loosened his hold on her and eventually stepped back.

'Don't say things like that.'

'Sorry.' He nodded. 'Quite right. Uh…so do you need to get ready for house calls?'

'Yes.'

'Go do that. I'll take care of the dishes.'

'And I need to clean Charlie's cage and change his water.'

'I can do that, too. Robby can help me.'

Aracely hesitated, about to tell him that she could cope, when Trent levelled a glare at her. 'Accept the help,' he reminded her softly. 'That's what you and I are going to do from now on. Accept help when people offer it.'

'It's not easy.'

'But we're used to being challenged,' he added, putting a positive spin on it.

'True. OK. You do the dishes and clean the bird's cage and I'll go get ready.'

'Done,' he agreed, and turned to his duties, listening to her walk down the hallway. Stepping out, accepting help definitely wasn't easy, not after what he'd been through. Even growing up in such a large family, it had usually been left to him to do the helping rather than being the one who asked for help. As the years had gone by, Trent had naturally slipped into a leadership role where his siblings and cousins were concerned, and a lot of the time he'd also borne the consequences when it had been someone else's fault.

When his marriage had come to an end, his siblings and extended family siding with Tessa rather than him, Trent had withdrawn, locked himself away in his work where he knew right from right and wrong from wrong. His parents had tried reaching out to him but he'd blocked them at every turn.

'Oops,' Aracely said, coming back into the kitchen. 'Found a glass in my bedroom.'

'That's fine,' he said, and added it to the dishes. Aracely smiled her thanks but instinctively realised something had changed in the few minutes she'd been gone.

'Is something wrong?' Was he regretting offering his help?

'No.' He paused. 'Well, not really. I was…just thinking about how I find it hard to accept help.'

'Oh.' She silently willed him to tell her, to open up a bit more, to take a chance and trust her. Her feet were glued to the spot and she found it impossible to move. 'Do you think you could tell me?' she asked slowly. 'I mean, I don't want to pry but—'

'I've told you my wife had an affair but what I didn't tell you was that she had it with my cousin,' he stated, and Aracely blinked, absorbing his words.

'Trent.' She put her hand on his arm and was pleased when he didn't brush her away.

'And while you think that might be enough, there's more. Much more.' He took a deep breath in before slowly letting it out. 'Tessa was pregnant.'

'Oh.' That was unexpected. Aracely frowned. 'But I thought you said you didn't have children.'

'*I* don't.'

'Ooh.' Her lips formed a circle as dawning realisation struck. 'It was your cousin's.'

'Although for the first six months of her pregnancy, she led me to believe it was mine.'

Aracely's heart bled for him and she tightened her grip on his arm, feeling the tension there. 'That must have… ' She trailed off, wanting to hold him close and offer all the comfort she could give.

'Hurt?' he supplied. 'It did. I wanted children,

Tessa didn't. When she became pregnant, she ranted and raved for the first eight weeks, threatening to get rid of it. I made a lot of rash promises, anything and everything just to get her to keep it. She was so mad. More mad at me than mad at being pregnant. Then when she went for her ultrasound, which she forbade me to attend, she found out she was a little further on than she'd originally thought. Of course, she continued to almost blackmail me out of money, property—whatever she could get—for the next few months, and she probably would have done right up until the baby's birth.'

'What happened?'

'My cousin couldn't take it any longer. He showed up, told me the truth. Said he couldn't go on lying to me and provided proof of paternity. He admitted to the affair, which had been going on a good half a year *before* she'd fallen pregnant. But it wasn't out of any guilt or concern that he told me. He was just mad Tessa wouldn't leave me for him and decided to force the issue. He was jealous. Pure and simple.'

Aracely couldn't believe what he was telling

her. This time she didn't hesitate and stepped forward to wrap her arms around him. He seemed initially startled by her contact but also accepted that this embrace didn't have anything to do with the attraction between them. It was one person offering comfort and support to another, and until that moment he realised no one else had offered him either during the past four years. Not like this.

They stood there, simply holding each other for a few minutes, before she eventually pulled away and kissed his cheek. 'Thank you for trusting me.'

Trent shrugged. 'You're an easy person to trust.'

'Perhaps because I've been through my own misery.'

'No. It's because you're an exceptional person, Aracely.'

'Hey, Mummy!' Robby yelled through the house. 'Where are my shoes?'

Aracely smiled at Trent. 'And you're an exceptional mummy.'

'Coming,' she called, but hesitated. 'I mean it, Trent. Thank you.'

He nodded. 'Go on. I've got a dishwasher to put on and a bird cage to clean.' As she left for the second time, he felt an enormous weight lift off him. He couldn't remember the last time he'd told anyone about his past and somehow telling Aracely all the gritty details had been like a cleansing. Or perhaps it was because she'd simply listened and then offered comfort. She hadn't given advice or her opinion, she'd just accepted.

Trent closed the dishwasher and thought of his family. How accepting was he of them? The last conversation he'd had with his mother, she'd been inviting him to a family party but Trent had known Tessa would be there…along with her husband—his cousin—and their four-year-old daughter. He'd been unable to do it and so when Dan, Greg and Phil had suggested going on a fishing trip, he'd readily agreed. Needing to get away. Now, though, for some reason, the thought of returning to the spiteful-ness of his extended family didn't seem to bother him as much and he knew the answer was Aracely. In the short time he'd known her, he'd changed…grown somehow…and the past, the pain which he'd locked there, was nowhere near as bad as it had been before.

Trent hardly spoke as Aracely drove to her first patient's house. When she'd left him in the kitchen he'd been all jovial and happy. Indeed, she'd heard both Trent and Robby laughing together as they'd cleaned out the bird's cage so why was he now so…withdrawn?

'Is something wrong?' she finally ventured.

'Huh? No. No. Nothing's wrong. Just thinking.'

'Deep thinking.'

He smiled. 'Yes. Sorry. So, tell me. Who's first on your list?' he asked as she pulled into a driveway and cut the engine. Trent looked at the old weatherboard home, the paint peeling off the sides, a large triangular antenna tower at the end of the driveway, the front garden a mix of roses, garden gnomes and weeds.

'Mrs Binks.'

'And why are you visiting Mrs Binks?' Trent asked as they both climbed from the vehicle, Aracely retrieving her backpack from the back seat.

'Angina.'

'She can't make it to the clinic for regular testing?' Trent asked as they walked to the front door.

'She also suffers from mild but increasing agoraphobia.'

'Interesting.' In the next instant the door was opened and Aracely smiled. 'Good morning, Matilda. I'm sorry I'm running a bit late. This is my colleague, Dr Trent Mornington.'

'Oh. Oh.' Matilda dithered as they entered her house. 'If I'd known you were bringing company, Doctor, I'd have tidied up a bit more.'

'Mrs Binks.' Trent addressed the elderly woman with natural friendliness. 'I have come to meet you, not your house, but I do apologise for any uneasiness I've caused.' He glanced around her cluttered living room, taking in the walls lined with photographs, the knick-knacks filling every available part of shelf space and the warm gas fire in the far wall. 'Besides, your home has a welcoming, cosy atmosphere. You don't find places like this in the city.'

Matilda Binks pressed her hand to her chest.

'Oh, Dr Mornington, do call me Matilda.' She smiled brightly at him. 'Oh, Dr Smith, you didn't say what a charmer he was. Oh, do come in. Come in and sit down right here, Dr Mornington. That was my late husband's favourite chair and I don't often let people sit in it, do I, now, Dr Smith?'

'No, you don't, Matilda. Quite an honour for you, Dr Mornington,' she said, amused at how taken her elderly patient was with Trent. 'Now,' she said, sitting down, 'how have you been feeling? Survived the storm all right?'

'Oh, yes, dear. My word, yes. What a night. What a frightful night it was. We haven't had a storm like that in a long time now. Poor Mr Chapman, though. It's a shame, isn't it?'

'Yes, but he's slowly improving and it could have been much worse.'

'And now he's staying at Emily Edmonson's house. Hmm,' Matilda fumed. 'Typical of that Emily Edmonson. Always sticking her nose in where it doesn't belong.' She frowned and then leaned forward towards Trent and said in a gossiping whisper, 'I've known Emily since we were girls and she always was a busybody.'

'She's his neighbour, Matilda. It's very kind of her to take him in.'

'Kind. Well, that's what some would call it. Kind. Ha! More like she wants to get her claws into him.'

Aracely hid her smile, recalling that Mr Chapman was considered one of the most eligible bachelors in Port Wallaby. 'Well, anyway, I'm pleased Winston is safe and wasn't too badly hurt.'

'Yes.' Matilda softened. 'I was so relieved when Jean called and passed on the news. I'd go and visit him myself if it weren't for…well, you know, dear. I like to stay close to home but I've already made him a nice casserole. Would you mind taking it around for me, Doctor?'

'I'd be delighted to.'

'If Winston needs to get out of *her* house, he can come and stay here. I don't mind. I'm very good at nursing people. Was a nurse's aide in the war, I was, and I nursed my Earl.'

'I remember you telling me.' Aracely looked over at Trent and found him watching the two of them closely, a twinkle of laughter in his eyes. 'Let's get your check-up started.'

Matilda clutched her hand to the top button of her blouse, glancing across at Trent, her eyes growing wide with alarm. Usually, as Matilda lived alone, they did the check-up here in the living room but although Trent was a doctor, the elderly lady wasn't about to unbutton anything in front of him.

'How about we do it in the bedroom today?' Aracely suggested, and her patient sighed with relief. 'Back in a moment,' Aracely said as the two of them disappeared. Trent wasn't quite sure what to do next and so stood, hitting his head on the low hanging light, grumbling as he rubbed his head and walked over to take a closer look at the photographs.

They told a story, the story of Matilda Binks's life, as they ranged from black and white photographs of people in wedding finery, right through to the woman herself surrounded by what he assumed were her fifteen grandchildren. It was the story of a family—a real family. He couldn't remember seeing this many pictures in his parents' home or even those of his uncles and aunts. No. This place, he thought as he looked at the cosy atmosphere, this place was a true home. He was sure that if the walls could speak, they would tell of love and laughter, of happy times and sad. It was the type of place he'd wanted for himself, a house that was a real home.

Aracely's home was like that. Although it was more spacious and less cluttered than Matilda's, it was warm and inviting and he'd immediately felt comfortable there. How had she made such a large place—even with her consulting rooms down at the rear of the house—into a loving haven where he always knew he'd be welcome? It was a gift, he eventually decided. One which Mrs Binks obviously shared, he thought as he picked up a ceramic unicorn from the shelf.

'That's one my Earl gave me for our fortieth wedding anniversary,' Matilda said as they returned. 'It may be cheap but the sentiment is there. He died not long after so it's a very special one.'

'It's lovely.' Trent replaced it. 'And how did the check-up go?' He looked to Aracely for his answer.

'She's doing just fine.' Aracely packed her

things away and went to lift the backpack up onto her shoulder when Trent took it out of her hands.

'I'll take it,' he said.

'Ah, now, isn't that just like a gentleman. I was just saying to Dr Smith here that you seemed like a lovely gentleman and she shouldn't let you escape. I said she should think seriously about getting you to stay in town because, goodness knows, we need another doctor and poor old Dr Baker can't keep helping out every time the town get hits with flu—or a storm as the case may be.'

'Right. Thank you, Matilda.' Aracely hurried towards the door. 'You rest now. The district nurse should be around to see you tomorrow.'

'All right, dear. Oh, and don't forget to take that casserole to poor Mr Chapman. I'll get it. It's in the kitchen. Won't be a minute, dear.'

When she was out of the room, Trent turned to Aracely. 'Who's Dr Baker?'

'Retired GP.'

'Who helps out when necessary.' Trent nodded. 'Well, then, it's just as well I'm going to hang around. That way Dr Baker can continue to enjoy his retirement.'

'Here you are, dear. I've wrapped it in a tea towel to keep it steady. It's a beef one. Winston's favourite.' She held it out to Aracely but again Trent intercepted it. 'Oh, thank you, Dr Mornington.' She giggled again. 'Such a gentleman.'

'My pleasure. I hope we'll be able to meet again while I'm here,' he said, and Aracely was surprised he didn't bow from the waist or lift Matilda's hand to his lips for a kiss.

'Oh, my. Well, you make sure Dr Smith brings you. Next time I'll have the kettle on and we can enjoy a nice cuppa.'

'Sounds delightful.'

Aracely opened the door. 'I'll let you know what's happening with the district nurse,' she said. 'Bye for now.' She pulled out her car keys and headed towards her car.

'And you make sure Emily Edmonson doesn't get her hands on that casserole. It's not for her,' Matilda called crossly from the doorway. She had the front door almost closed on her face, as though she were too frightened to come outside but wanted desperately to get her point across.

'We will,' Aracely said as they climbed into the

car. 'Bye.' She started the engine and reversed, waving to Matilda as they drove off.

'So? How did you enjoy your first house call?' she asked.

'Interesting. Very interesting. It's different actually being invited into someone's life like that, to see how they live, what their houses are like.'

'Matilda is unique, I'll give you that. I love all those photos of hers. Usually, because I have a bit more time, we have a cup of tea and she'll tell me a story about one of them or an anecdote from her past. It's nice.'

'Sounds like it.'

'What about you?'

'Me? What about me?'

'Aren't you going to tell me some anecdotes from your life? I mean, so many brothers and sisters. You're bound to have a few hair-raising stories.'

'Hair-raising is right.' The smile that came to his face was easy and familiar and Aracely was glad to see him relaxing. 'Caroline—who is the youngest girl—decided to dye her hair when she was about twelve, I think. My parents were both at work, I was in charge after school and so naturally I was the one who got into the most trouble.'

'What did she do?'

'Well, somehow she got the idea she could dye her hair by using the food colouring Mum had in the cupboard. Unfortunately, she decided to use the red hair dye and let me tell you—that doesn't really come off bathroom tiles all that easily. It also looked like blood and so when Mum walked into the bathroom that evening, she screamed the place down.'

Aracely couldn't help but laugh. 'And Caroline?'

'She had red dye everywhere. Her face, her ears, down her neck, her hands and fingers, not to mention all over her clothes. Took ages to grow out as well.' His eyes were twinkling at the memory but as she turned the corner, she realised that the laughter was disappearing fast.

'When was the last time you saw Caroline?'

Trent swallowed. 'The day after my divorce. You see, Caroline and my ex-wife are best friends.'

'Ah.'

Again, as he spoke the pain he'd always experienced didn't come and it had him thinking again.

What had changed? Why could he now think of his family without the suffering of the last few years?

Aracely turned into the street where Mr Chapman had lived and was surprised at how well the clean-up was going.

'Wow. They've really cleaned up the street,' Trent commented, as Aracely pulled her car into Mrs Edmonson's driveway.

They both got out and stood on the front lawn, looking across the street to the rubble where Winston's house used to be. 'I've heard of things like this happening but I've never seen it with my own eyes.'

'What's that?'

'A storm or a fire or a cyclone hitting one house but not another.'

Aracely nodded. 'It's pretty freaky.'

'You can say that again.'

'It's pretty freaky,' she repeated, as they walked up Mrs Edmonson's front path.

'Funny.' His tone was laconic.

'I'm a funny woman,' she drawled seriously, as she pressed the doorbell.

A moment later the door was opened in a rush

of words. 'Doctor, there you are. Thank goodness you've come.' Mrs Edmonson reached for Aracely's hand, tugging her inside. She continued chatting non-stop as she led them upstairs to where Mr Chapman was staying.

As Emily put her hand on the doorknob of the spare room, Trent noticed her hands were red, raw pink and his mind immediately came up with three different diagnoses. Was the woman's constant chatter her way of covering her nervousness? Was there something deeper going on here? He glanced at Aracely, wondering if she was picking up the same things as him. Then again, she probably knew everything about these people, about what was going on in their lives. Trent had heard that a lot of country GPs also became therapists of a sort, someone people could turn to in times of need, knowing their confidences would be kept. That would be Aracely.

'Winston.' Aracely shook her head in worry as she headed over to her patient. Trent put the casserole dish down on top of a tallboy and watched as Aracely took the man's bandaged hands carefully in hers and looked into his eyes with empathy and understanding. 'How are you feeling today?'

And there it was. Her naturally caring attitude, which somehow made everyone she treated feel one hundred per cent special. As though they were her only patient, as though she would do anything and everything for them to see them through their recovery or illness or whatever. Perhaps it was because she'd been through her own private pain with her accident and no doubt hindered her own recovery.

Trent walked carefully around to the other side of the patient, Mr Chapman greeting him like an old friend.

'Let's see how your hands are today,' she said as she unwrapped the bandages. 'The painkillers still working all right?'

'Perfect, Doc.'

'I don't know about that, Dr Smith,' Mrs Edmonson interjected from her position next to the door. 'As I've said, he's been complaining of headaches and he's been awfully tired. Now, I don't want to overstep my bonds of neighbourly hospitality, but—'

'Emily,' Aracely interrupted firmly but politely. 'I have some tablets here for Winston and I see that his water glass is empty. I wonder if you'd be so kind as to fetch a glass of water, please. I'd appreciate it.'

'So would I,' Winston said under his breath.

'Of course,' Emily said with the utmost assurance and rushed from the room.

'That woman can talk the hind leg off a donkey,' Winston grumbled, and Aracely didn't try to hide her smile. 'Headaches, she says. Too right I've been having headaches, Doc. She doesn't keep quiet. You've gotta get me out of here.'

'Be good and I'll see what I can do. Now, let's take a good look at you.' She examined his hands and was pleased with the mild improvement since yesterday. She withdrew fresh bandages and rewrapped his hands. 'Do you have pain anywhere else? Anywhere besides your head, of course,' she clarified.

'The back of my neck,' he said, and winced when she touched it. 'Every time I move. Think I might have done some muscle damage.'

'Trent?' Aracely called, and moved aside so he

could get closer. 'Trent is an orthopaedic surgeon,' she explained. 'The perfect person to check your neck as he's had far more experience with bones and muscles than I have.'

Trent appreciated her words and stepped forward to examine Mr Chapman. He pressed on the back of the shoulder and the neck with only minor effect but when he moved around to the front of the neck, Winston winced again.

'Feels as though you might have fractured your clavicle,' he said, touching the collar-bone.

'When did the pain start?' Aracely asked.

'It's been there all along but I guess I haven't been that aware of it.'

'The pain medication was probably masking it.' Trent nodded.

'Do you think I need transferring to Moonta? A few days in a nice quiet hospital?' Winston asked hopefully.

'They're all full up after the storm.' Aracely noticed the pleading in his eyes. 'Wallaroo hospital, for that matter, too, but I'll see what I can organise. At the least I want you brought to my clinic so I can X-ray you.'

'Is there someone else you can stay with for a few days?' Trent asked.

'Possibly,' Winston said. 'But I don't like to put people out. After the storm, everyone's got their own problems.'

'We'll get you sorted out,' she said to him as she packed away her stethoscope and took out another packet of pills. 'You'll need to take one of these morning, noon and night, with food, for the next few days at least. It's for the infection. The antibiotics I put you on the other day don't seem to be doing the trick.'

'Righto,' Winston answered. When Mrs Edmonson returned, he had swallowed his tablet.

'Emily,' Aracely began. 'We'll need to take Winston with us, back to my clinic for X-rays. Dr Baker's agreed to let Winston stay with him for a few days as he may have a reaction to the new medicine I've just put him on.'

'I can take him anywhere he needs to be,' Emily offered, and Aracely instantly felt bad for her. Crossing to her side, she put her right hand on the woman's shoulder.

'You've done a fantastic job of looking after

him, and I for one am grateful, as I'm sure Winston is.'

Winston nodded his head obediently.

'He does need further medical treatment and I know Dr Baker won't mind. Besides, I've heard from several patients that the relief effort for those affected worst by the storm throughout the peninsula is in full swing. In fact, Dorothea was only telling me yesterday how she was hoping to secure you as one of the co-ordinators.'

'Well, yes, she did call.' Emily preened a little. 'I wasn't sure what to say, as I already had duties to attend to here.' She indicated Winston as she spoke.

'Now your time is once again your own and I know you'll put it to good use.' Aracely's words were heartfelt. Emily Edmonson was an obsessive, compulsive cleaner, the current state of her hands was testimony of that, yet if she was physically busy, things tended to calm down a little.

'Yes. Yes, you're right, Dr Smith. I'll call Dorothea this instant.' With that, she left the room and a moment later Winston gave a whoop of joy, then immediately winced in pain.

'You're a miracle-worker, Doc. That's what you are.'

Aracely sighed as she packed her things up. 'Let's get you back to my clinic for X-rays, Winston, then we'll get you settled with Dr Baker.'

'Dr Baker won't mind?' Trent asked after they'd said goodbye to Mrs Edmonson and settled Winston in the back of Aracely's car.

'Not in the slightest. The two men are good friends and, besides, it was Dr Baker's idea when he called to discuss the situation with me yesterday.'

'Really? When?'

'During clinic. Something wrong?'

Trent slowly shook his head. 'So you're a social worker, too? Counsellor? What other hats do you wear, Aracely?'

'Oh, you name it, I've worn it.' She pointed to the crockery pot he still cradled and smiled. 'Meals on wheels.'

'And so you usually organise your patients' lives?'

'If it's going to affect their healing, yes. That's part of my job.'

'Hmm. I'd never thought of it that way before.' Trent continued to ponder as she drove back to her clinic. They X-rayed Winston's clavicle and indeed found it broken, as well as discovering a few hairline fractures of his ribs. They strapped him up and then transferred him to Dr Baker's house.

'I'm much obliged,' Winston said. 'And you've even transported my casserole for me.'

'Dinner?' George Baker said, lifting the lid and sighing at the glorious smell. 'Excellent. With Innis off in Adelaide, missing the storm of the century, I've been bach-ing it.'

'You can thank Matilda Binks for your dinner, then.' Aracely and Trent left the two bachelors to themselves.

'Is Uncle Robert next on the list?' Trent asked. 'Robby assured me he was.'

'Yes, but there's a few things you—' She broke off as her phone rang. She pressed the connection for the hands-free speaker. 'Dr Smith.'

'Cely.' Billy's voice came down the line—and it was clear he was worried. 'It's Maggie. Come back. Come back now. She's in pain!'

CHAPTER TEN

ARACELY swung the car around and headed back towards her house. 'Talk to me, Billy. What's going on?'

'She just has pain. Really bad cramps.'

'Any bleeding?'

There was a pause. 'No.'

Aracely could hear Robby crying in the background and Maggie trying to placate him. 'That's a good sign. No blood is a good sign. Put her in the recovery position if you can, or just get her as comfortable as you can. We're about three minutes away.'

Her mind was whirling out of control, trying to sort through different scenarios and possibilities, but also she couldn't help the emotional pain at the thought that her sister might lose another baby. She wanted to scream and rant and rave and cry, but she was driving and keeping a cool, clear head was paramount.

'Is she having leg cramps?' Trent asked.

'Yes,' came Billy's reply.

'Is it severe? Consistent?' Trent continued with the questions. He'd taken one look at Aracely and seen the colour drain from her face. The line between doctor and sister was starting to blur. He was there to help her, so help her he would.

'There's no spotting? No spotting at all?'

'No,' came Billy's reply once more.

'Has she vomited? Voided?' Aracely spoke.

'No.'

'We're here,' she said and disconnected the call, her feet hitting the ground running as she headed straight for her sister's house. The instant she stepped inside, Robby hurled himself at her and she gathered him up, holding him close and wiping away his tears.

'Is Aunty Maggie going to be all right?'

'I hope so, darling,' she said. 'Is she in the bedroom?' She headed up the hallway, knowing Trent was behind her every step of the way. She couldn't see him but she could sense him, feel him, and it was such comforting reassurance to know there was another medically trained person with her right at this moment. If she forgot something, if she failed to pick up anything important, she knew she'd never forgive herself. This was her sister she was treating and that brought with it all sorts of emotional complications.

When she saw her sister lying on the bed, silent tears trickling down her cheeks, Aracely's own eyes misted over immediately. 'Oh, Maggie. What's happened?' She managed to unwind Robby's arms from her neck. 'Darling,' she said to her son. 'Mummy needs to look at Aunty Maggie.'

'I don't want to go,' he said.

'Can you sit over there on the chair? You'll need to be quiet.'

'OK.' He did as he was told and Trent saw he already had Mr Rabbit in his hands for comfort. When the little boy's lower lip began to wobble, his heart lurched. Such a caring, sensitive little boy. Aracely had done an excellent job of raising him.

'What type of pain is it? Where?' She sat carefully on the edge of the bed and put her hand on her sister's abdomen. Trent was pulling out the sphygmomanometer, getting ready to check Maggie's BP. Billy shifted momentarily from his wife's side to give him access.

'I was lying down, resting like you'd told me to, and then when I went to get up…it was so sharp and so stabbing.'

'Like pain you've had before?' Aracely asked.

'No. It's different. This is the longest I've ever carried a baby, Cely.' The tears began again. 'I can't lose this one. I've been good. I've been doing everything right. I've been resting.'

'Don't cry, Aunty Maggie,' Robby called, his voice distraught with worry.

'She's all right, darling,' Aracely placated. 'Sometimes when women have babies in their tummies their feelings go a little crazy and that makes them cry more than usual.'

'BP's slightly elevated but otherwise you're doing fine, Maggie.'

'So the pain?'

'It was stabbing. Just here.' Maggie showed her the spot.

'Is it there now?'

Maggie thought for a moment. 'It feels as

though it's subsided.' Her eyes were wide as she mentally thought about the pain. 'Definitely not as bad as it was.'

'Right. Let's see if you can sit up. Slowly. Take it nice and easy.' With Billy supporting his wife, Maggie was able to sit up, although still quite gingerly.

'Ligament pain?' Trent looked at Aracely.

'Sounds like it.'

'Ligament pain? That doesn't sound serious,' Billy commented.

'It isn't.' Aracely sighed as Maggie was now able to stand and walk slowly around the room without any further pain.

'Yay. You're better. My mummy fixed you.' Robby was out of his chair and ran to stand between his two favourite women. Aracely picked him up and kissed him, hugging him close.

'Ligament pain is something pregnant women experience in their second trimester,' she announced with a bright smile.

'What? You mean I'm really OK?' Maggie couldn't believe it.

'Looks that way to me.'

'I feel like such a fool.'

'No. Never that.' Aracely shifted Robby to her hip and hugged her sister with her free arm. 'You've never carried this far before so it's only natural that you'd be concerned, especially with what you've been through in the past.'

'So why is she having the pain?' Billy asked.

'Stretching.' Trent shrugged. 'The ligaments that support the uterus are stretching and becoming thick so they can support its enlargement as the baby grows.'

'Making more room.' Aracely couldn't believe how amazingly happy she felt. She let go of Maggie and tossed Robby, who was holding Mr Rabbit, in the air. 'Because babies like to grow bigger and bigger and the mummy's tummy stretches and ligaments stretch and all too soon, you, my son, are going to have a cousin.' Robby giggled and squealed with delight as she caught him and tickled him. Now that his world was right again, Robby wriggled free and headed down the hallway.

'However,' Aracely cautioned, 'if they're persistent and last a long time—like a minute or more—you are to call me instantly,' she warned her sister.

'Don't you worry. You'll know of every twinge.'

'Good.' Heaving another huge sigh of relief, Aracely smiled at Trent. 'I think our work here is done. I think I'll take Robby off your hands as well.'

'It's all right,' Maggie protested.

'He can come with us for the rest of the day. I've got three more house calls scheduled and one of them is Uncle Robert.'

'OK, then.'

'And don't worry about making dinner tonight,' Trent said. 'I can take care of it.'

Maggie raised her eyebrows questioningly. 'Like you took care of breakfast? I heard all about the pancakes.'

Trent grimaced mockingly. 'Oops. Well, I promise you, it won't be pancakes for dinner.'

'So long as it's healthy. My sister needs to maintain her strength and not through junk food.'

'Where I'm a conservation nut, Maggie's a healthy-eating nut,' Aracely supplied.

'I'd guessed that already,' Trent remarked.

'Welcome to the madhouse of the Smith sisters.' Billy rolled his eyes but quickly kissed his wife before she could hit him.

'You rest,' Aracely told her sister as they headed out. 'Come on, Robby. Get your things. You can come out to see Uncle Robert with us.'

'Yay!'

They went to Aracely's house where she re-stocked her backpack while Trent made sandwiches for lunch. 'You're quite the gourmet,' she stated, taking her second sandwich. 'Vegemite. My favourite.'

Trent laughed and she let the sound wash over her. He'd been there for only a few days and already it was starting to feel as though he belonged here. Not only here in Port Wallaby, not only helping her in her medical practice, but right here, as an integral part of her life. Robby climbed up onto his knee and Trent immediately accommodated him. Aracely knew, from the few things he'd already said, that his divorce hadn't been an amicable one. Those were rare. She knew he'd locked himself away in his work and was now trying something new and she admired him for it.

'You'd make a wonderful father.' The words came out of her mouth before she'd really had time to think about it and she immediately hoped he wouldn't take them the wrong way. Did he think she was sizing him up as a father for Robby? Aracely frowned for a moment. Well, was she? Not knowing the answer herself, she decided that, instead of trying to explain her statement, she'd just let it go and forget about it.

'Thank you.' He dropped a casual kiss on her son's head and Aracely's heart turned over at the sight. Robby simply accepted the affection but, then, her son thought it unusual if people *didn't* fawn all over him. In Robby's eyes he was irresistible and he knew it.

Aracely swallowed the last bite of her sandwich. 'We'd better get started.'

The rest of her house-call list went a lot smoother than the morning's and just before four o'clock she pulled into Uncle Robert's driveway. Robby was out of the car like a shot, leaving his mother and Trent to follow at a slower pace. 'I just need to warn you. Uncle Robert is old. He's cantankerous and he's the most delightful man in my life, save my son—who you might have guessed was named after him. He'll ask you all sorts of personal questions but if you feel uncomfortable or don't want to—'

'Aracely.' Trent stopped her, pressing a finger lightly to her lips. 'Shh. I can handle it.' As though he realised just how close they were, he quickly removed his finger but it was too late. There was an imprint where he'd touched her and her body was starting to burn with heightened awareness once more. She forced herself to move away from him lest she grab him and press her mouth to his that instant, which was what she was dying to do.

'You coming in or not?' Uncle Robert's voice came from inside the house. 'In or out but close the door. You're letting all the bought air out and I'm not made of money, girlie.'

Aracely smiled. 'Don't say I didn't warn you.'

'Who are you?' Uncle Robert barked when he saw Trent.

'This is—' Aracely began, but Trent quickly put out his hand introduced himself.

'Trent Mornington, sir. Pleased to meet you.'

'I ain't no *sir,*' Uncle Robert began. 'I've been a working man all my life, boy.'

'Of course.' Trent nodded solemnly, knowing full well that Aracely was trying not to laugh.

'Be nice,' she warned. 'Now, have you been taking your tablets?'

'Why do you ask me those sorts of questions every time you come? Why can't you ask me something different?'

'Such as?'

'How many beers have I guzzled? What have I been planting in my garden? How much fried food have I stuffed into me mouth? You know, that sort of thing.'

'You had better not have been doing any of those things—well, except for the gardening and even then you need to take it easy,' Aracely lectured. She picked up his pills and tipped the contents out onto the table and began counting.

'What are you doing?'

'Answering the question you wouldn't.'

'You've been keeping count of my pills?'

'Yes.' She raised her eyebrows. 'Sly, aren't I?'

'If I'd known, I'd have flushed a few down the sink.'

'They're all here. You haven't taken any since I saw you last, have you?' she accused, and although her tone was brisk it was also filled with love and concern. Trent also thought he heard a thread of fear.

Uncle Robert turned away and directed his comments to Trent. 'A man should be allowed to die when he chooses, don't you agree?'

'I'm a doctor and as such I've sworn an oath to uphold and protect life—just as Aracely has.' He almost added *sir* on the end but quickly stopped himself.

'Well, you're useless, then.' He looked back at his niece. 'Let me go, darlin',' he said softly, and held out a hand to her. Aracely took it, unable to be cross with him for more than a second.

'I can't.' She squeezed his hand before letting it go.

'Where are you going?' Robby asked, and climbed up onto the old man's knee. 'Can I come, too?'

Uncle Robert closed his tired arms around the

boy. 'No, son. This is a one-way trip for your old Uncle Robert.'

The room was silent, so silent Trent could hear the wind whirling around outside. Aracely's eyes were filled with tears and he watched her try to suppress them. He reached for her hand and held it, offering his reassurance and support. He couldn't say what prompted him to do it, it simply felt right.

'All right. I'll take the tablets,' Uncle Robert finally said. 'But only because I don't want the staff here to be bugging me all the time. You're bad enough, Cely.'

'I'll take the tablets, too,' Robby offered. 'You don't need to be scared of them, Uncle Robert.'

The old man laughed heartily and ruffled the boy's hair. It was enough to break the sombre atmosphere. 'You're a delight, boy,' he told the four-year-old. 'Just like your mother and your aunt.'

With the situation now diffused, they stayed for a few more minutes before Aracely kissed Uncle Robert's cheek. 'I'll see you tomorrow.'

He nodded but didn't say anything else until Trent and Robby had headed to the car. 'Cely,' he said, calling her back. 'He's a good man. He cares—deeply.'

'You can tell that from a brief meeting.'

'A man's eyes—a *true* man's eyes—never lie. I've met too many people and I know a deceptive person when I meet them, even if it's for a minute or two. He's a good man,' Uncle Robert reiterated. 'Had his fair share of knocks but he's a good man, Cely. Hang onto this one.'

She opened her mouth to speak but he stopped her, placing a hand on her shoulder. 'Not now,' he said, and she could see he was exhausted.

'Rest.'

'Yes.'

Thankfully Robby was there to chatter his way through the drive back home. He chattered when they stopped off at the supermarket to pick up ingredients for the meal Trent was going to cook and he chattered all through their barbecue dinner. Usually at this time of night Aracely found her son's constant chatter wearing down her nerves but tonight she was glad of it. Her own mood was too melancholy and once she'd finally settled her son for the night, she said goodnight to Trent and hibernated in her room.

She was still withdrawn the following morning, Trent noted as they ate breakfast at the table together. She had a clinic on in the morning and was more than happy to accept Trent's offer to look after Robby. She went out alone for her afternoon house calls and seemed even more depressed when she returned. Again, she avoided him in the evening and by Sunday evening, he couldn't take it any longer.

'Do you want to talk about it?'

'About what?' She sniffed and blew her nose, her head feeling as though it weighed a ton.

'Whatever is bothering you. I presume it's your uncle?'

Her sigh was heavy as she drained the last of her herbal tea, glad Robby had gone to sleep quite quickly tonight. 'That's part of it.'

'What's the other part?'

'That I feel drained. That at the moment I don't have the strength to cope with anything. My head hurts, my arms and legs ache and my nose won't stop running.'

'You're getting sick.'

'No. I never get sick.'

'Hmm.' He watched her for another minute. 'Aracely, if you want to talk, I'm here for you. Ready to listen if you just want to vent. Talking about things might help lift some of that heaviness you're feeling. I should know. I won't offer advice unless it's asked and even then I'll do so very cautiously.'

She smiled at him for the first time in days and his heart lifted in pleasure. 'All right, then.'

'OK. Let's sit down.' With that, he took her hand and led her to the sofa. They sat facing each other, Trent still holding her hand in his. He didn't prompt her or force her to start talking. Instead he merely waited until she was ready and Aracely knew Uncle Robert was right. Trent *was* a good man.

'I usually talk to Maggie about…well, everything, but at the moment I think she's got enough to cope with.'

He nodded and continued to wait.

'Uncle Robert's dying. I know it. I can see it. I can even understand it.' She shook her head.

'But I don't want it. I mean, the man's ninety-four and the fact that he says he's ready to go scares me completely.'

'That's understandable. I take it he's been a constant in your life.'

'Yes. I'm named after his sister. My son is named after him. We're connected. More so than Maggie is. It's hard to explain.'

'Your bond is strong,' he stated.

'Exactly.'

'So what else is bothering you?' he asked after a moment's pause.

Aracely let out a long sigh and shifted among the cushions before looking him straight in the eyes. 'You.'

'Ah.'

'You're a good man, Trent.'

'Thank you.'

'But there are so many uncertainties where you're concerned.' She pushed her hair from her face with her free hand. 'I don't know whether I'm up or down. I admire you, not only as a doctor but as a person, as a man—as a man I could become involved with, and that's just too dangerous.'

He was silent at her words and she half wished him to say something but he didn't.

'I've been hurt before and so have you,' she eventually continued. 'We've both agreed there's chemistry between us and while that's all well and good…' She trailed off, shaking her head. 'I live here. I have my life here with Robby. You have a life somewhere else.'

'Well, it depends what your definition of the word *life* is. I work in Sydney. Since coming to Port Wallaby, I've begun to realise that that's about all. I work in Sydney but I'm not sure I live there.'

Aracely frowned. 'I don't understand.'

'I don't expect you to.' He dropped her hand but didn't move. Instead he reached out and touched her hair, Aracely thrilling at the touch. 'I'm a very private person, Cely. I guess it comes from having so many siblings and people sticking their noses into my life. I've learned to keep myself to myself and in part I guess that was one of the reasons why my marriage failed.'

'You also said your wife was unfaithful,' she pointed out, not liking the way he seemed to be taking all the blame.

'Would she have been if I'd been more open?' He coiled a curl around his finger. 'That's a question that has plagued me for far too long.'

'It takes two to make a marriage work, Trent. We both know that.'

'Yes. It also takes a burning need to communicate, to *want* to let the other person into your deepest, most private place.' He shook his head sadly. 'I didn't want to let Tessa in. I can admit that now.'

'Why now?'

He shifted closer as he spoke, cradling her head in his hand. 'Because of you.'

'Me?' The word squeaked out.

'I have that burning need to communicate with you, Aracely. I want to open up to you and the urge for you to want to do the same with me is even stronger. I know it's not fair to ask you to talk to me, to confide in me, without giving something of myself in return.'

Aracely's breath whispered out between her parted lips as he edged even closer.

'Are you scared?' His voice was deep, soft and so rich it washed over her, capturing her and warming her through and through. Trent picked up her injured hand in his free one.

'No.' His scent was all around her, drawing her in, making her feel as though she were floating. He brought her hand to his lips and tenderly kissed the scars, Aracely gasping in response. 'You smell so good,' she whispered, and breathed in deeply to prove her point.

'You're making me crazy,' he countered, and brushed his thumb across her lips. 'I want to kiss you. I need to kiss you.' He shook his head softly and groaned with longing when her tongue flicked out to wet her lips, catching the tip of his thumb.

'You're making me crazy,' he mumbled again, as the decision to give in to temptation was made and accepted. Slowly, ever so slowly, Trent lowered his head towards her and Aracely's eyelids fluttered closed in breathless anticipation.

His mouth was close, so close to hers, their breath hanging in the air and mingling together. Aracely had never felt more alive in her entire life. Every nerve ending was tingling with excited apprehension and her impatience was increasing with each passing second.

Finally…finally, his lips tentatively touched hers and she released the breath she'd been unconsciously holding. He seemed to take that as a sign to continue.

The next kiss was no more than a long, glorious slide with a touch more pressure than the first. She started to tremble and wondered if he planned on making her as crazy for him as he'd said he was for her.

The third kiss was firmer, still testing the waters between them, but it was powerful enough for her pulse rate to shoot sky high at the tantalising feel of his mouth on hers. Slow motion enveloped them as he pressed his lips, once, twice, three times against hers. Then his tongue came out to begin its torture, tracing lightly across her lower lip before tilting upwards. A shudder of delight rippled through her and the need to hold him close, to ensure he didn't break this exquisite torture was paramount.

She shifted and brought her hands up to his neck, her fingers working their way around to the back before plunging into his soft hair, forcing his head down a little further.

'Mmm,' he moaned, and opened his mouth to deepen the kiss. She was exquisite, tasting of peppermints from her herbal tea and smelling like wild flowers. He'd wanted to kiss her like this since the first moment he'd initially touched his lips to hers. Thoughts of what it might be like to hold her to him, to feel her arms around him, his mouth on hers had plagued him. Now, though, he realised his imagination had been sadly lacking because the reality of her was far more than he'd ever dreamed of. She was…intoxicating.

His fingers at the back of her neck were rubbing in tiny circles, releasing endorphins which only served to enhance the way he was making her feel. When he temporarily pulled his mouth from hers, gasping for air, she knew she wasn't quite ready to let him go. He'd opened the door, she'd walked through it but now she wanted more.

'Trent,' she breathed. 'It's wild.'

'I know.' He shook his head and pressed butterfly kisses to her cheeks. 'I know.'

Logic and reason didn't appear to have any say in what they were feeling and when she urged his mouth back to hers, he went willingly.

Trent continued to luxuriate in the texture of her glorious soft curls and she moaned with delight at the feel of his hands in her hair, the way he gently massaged her scalp before trailing his fingers through the curls. He seemed to know exactly what to do to garner a response from her, a response she was more than willing to give. It made her wonder whether she could drive him as insane as he appeared determined to do to her.

Easing back slightly, she slowly trailed her hands down across his broad shoulders and came to rest on his chest. Her fingertips tingled on their journey and when she felt the contours of his body beneath his polo shirt, she realised that touching him in this intimate way affected her far more than it seemed to do for him.

A second later, though, a shudder ripped through him and she deepened the kiss, accepting his reaction into the heat they were generating between them. Given her success, she found her boldness increasing and moved her hands further down enjoying his reaction. When she came to his waist she found herself impatient and gently tugged the fabric from the waistband of his jeans.

He held his breath, his mouth still firmly on hers, but when her hands finally made contact with his skin, he groaned, releasing the pent-up air and plundering her mouth. She slid her hands around to his back, her nails scratching him lightly, which only succeeded in heightening his reaction to her touch.

Once more he gathered her to him, his mouth never wanting to leave, never wanting to stop what was happening between them. Never? Where had that come from? He wasn't the type of man to play with a woman's affections. Was this thing between them growing beyond what either of them expected? A relationship? Then what? Marriage?

At that thought Trent jerked back, gasping as he released her so abruptly she almost fell off the sofa. He placed his hands on her shoulders until she'd righted herself before dropping them back to his side.

'Trent?' Her breathing was as erratic as his but the questioning look in her eyes made him feel horrible. 'What's wrong?'

'Nothing.'

'Did I do something wrong?'

And there it was. Her insecurity and uncertainty. Her worry that all this was her fault. She'd been hurt before and no doubt made to feel as though she'd been responsible for everything that had gone wrong. He knew because that's exactly what had happened to him. As far as Tessa was concerned, it had all been his fault. He'd driven her to have the affair with his cousin. He'd forced her to lie to him about the baby. Trent shook his head.

'Cely.' She was starting to mean something to him, something important. 'I'm sorry.'

Aracely didn't move, trying to figure out exactly what he was sorry for. For kissing her? For showing her that those emotions she'd thought dormant or non-existent were very much alive and raring to go?

'Sorry? For what?' she asked, deciding to call him on it. 'For kissing me?'

Was he? The answer came fast. 'No. I'm not sorry for that.'

'Then what?'

'I didn't mean to make things more confusing

for you.' Or for himself, he added silently. 'I want us to get to know each other, to see where this attraction leads. When I spoke about communicating, I hadn't meant like that...although...' he grinned '...it does have its benefits.'

Aracely couldn't help but smile at his words. 'I know what you mean. We've both been hurt before. We're both cautious about putting ourselves out there again. I get that part but there's something else.'

Trent raked a hand through his hair. He's spoken about opening up and that was what he needed to do now. He cleared his throat. 'It's the intensity, which is why we need to get to know each other better. I leave at the end of next week to return to Sydney.' He took her hands in his, his words imploring. 'Would you agree to...date?'

'Date? For a week?'

'Yes. We talk, we be open with each other. We spend time together and with Robby.' A smile touched his lips at the mention of her son. 'He's amazing, Cely. You've done such a wonderful job with him.'

'I had good material to work with. Uncle

Robert says it's genetic that my son would be brilliant.' Aracely smiled. 'Personally, I think he was just trying to bolster his namesake.'

'So what do you say?'

Aracely shifted, thinking it over. She wanted to take a chance with him, to see what might happen.

'You can sleep on it. We can talk more in the morning,' he offered.

She chuckled. 'How could I possibly sleep with those types of thoughts running around in my head?' Then she looked into his warm brown eyes. 'I think it's a good idea. I mean, we need to at least try, right?'

Trent couldn't believe how relieved he felt at her words. 'Right.' With that, he stood and pulled her to her feet. 'Now that the decision's been made, go and get some sleep.'

'But I need to do the dishes and I haven't changed Charlie's water and I need to cover him and—'

'Go to bed, Aracely. I'll take care of it.' He drew her to him and placed a kiss on her forehead. 'Sleep sweet.'

Once she was ready for bed, she lay there, listening for sounds of Trent moving around the house as she thought about everything he'd said. He wanted to date! She couldn't remember another man ever asking her in such a way. It was almost as though he was declaring his intentions and she liked it. It was old-fashioned, showed he respected not only her but her son as well, and it also fitted with the picture she'd pieced together of him. Trent Mornington was a gentleman.

CHAPTER ELEVEN

WHEN Aracely woke the next morning it was to find her entire body feeling like lead. Wearily, she checked the time and knew she must still be dreaming as it was well after ten o'clock. Why hadn't her alarm gone off? With a heavy hand she checked it, positive she'd set it last night. It wasn't on. It was very odd.

Knowing she'd have a waiting room full of people wanting to see her, she stumbled out, coughing and blowing her nose as she pulled on whatever clothes were lying around. She caught her hair back in a band and with a box of tissues under her arm, she shuffled out of her room and down the hallway.

She stopped when she saw the full waiting room of people, all staring at her as though she had two heads. 'Sorry,' she mumbled, but even that word was broken by a sneeze. She blew her nose and crossed to her consulting room. 'Won't be a moment.' When she opened the door Aracely was stunned to find Trent sitting behind her desk, talking with Mrs Blythe.

He frowned when he saw her. 'What are you doing out of bed?' he said, excusing himself from his patient.

'What?' Aracely coughed.

'Stop spreading germs.' Trent placed his arm around Aracely and led her from the room. Stubbornly she stood her ground.

'What are you doing?'

'Your clinic. You're sick, Aracely. Now, back to bed with you.'

'I'm not sick. I'm never sick.'

'Sure.' Why did he sound as though he didn't believe her?

'And where's my son?'

'Robby is at preschool.' Trent tried to shift her again but once more she refused to budge. 'Hmm. I see you want to do things the hard way, eh?' Before Aracely had time to process his words, Trent had scooped her into his arms.

'Hey! What?' But as she spoke, his body warmth flooded through her and she was suddenly too overcome with the sensations he evoked to resist him.

'Back to bed, Dr Smith,' he murmured, pleased when her head dropped against his shoulder. He heard some of her patients gasp. One said, 'Oh, how romantic,' and another clapped with glee. Trent tightened his grip on her, liking the feeling of having her close to him, even if she was finding it difficult to breathe through her nose.

When he'd deposited her back in her bed, he pulled the covers up. 'Back in a moment.' Aracely closed her eyes and lay there. Trent returned with a glass of water and two little white pills. Without question she swallowed them, then rested back among the pillows.

'Now sleep,' he said. 'The sinus decongestion tablets will help your aches and pains as well as help you breathe more easily.' Trent bent and kissed her forehead, lingering a moment. 'You don't have a temperature, which is a good sign.' Brushing his fingers down her cheek, he whispered, 'Rest. I'll take care of everything.'

'Robby?'

'I'll get him from preschool, bring him back. He's fine. A little concerned about you but fine. Trust me, Cely. I won't let you down.'

'I know,' she mumbled as she snuggled into her covers. 'I'm glad you're here, Trent.'

Trent stood there for another minute just watching her unable to kick the powerful sensation of protective satisfaction he felt from being able to look after her. She was letting him help her, letting him in to her life—trusting him with not only her own well-being but that of her son and her patients.

He breathed in deeply before quietly leaving her in peace.

The next time she woke it was because someone was wriggling in the bed beside her. She put out a hand and encountered a small body.

'Mummy. You're awake!'

Aracely smiled, feeling much better than before. 'How was preschool?'

'Mrs Moody ran out of play dough and so I got to help her make some more and that was really fun and I got to choose the colours and I chose green 'cos it's my favourite and purple 'cos that's your favourite and blue 'cos that's Trent's favourite and all the kids liked the colours and said they were the best.' Robby bounced up and down on her bed as he spoke, excitement in his eyes.

'Come here,' she said, and pulled him close for a cuddle. He was still for about a minute before he broke free and climbed from the bed, thrusting Mr Rabbit into her neck.

'Here you go. Mr Rabbit will help you get better,' he said, and she accepted her son's loving gesture before Robby turned and raced from the room. 'She's awake, Trent,' he yelled. 'I told you she would wake up when I went in.'

Aracely smiled to herself and a moment later Trent appeared in her doorway, tall and looming as he'd appeared that first night on the beach. It seemed so long ago instead of only six days. Now, though, he didn't look frightening or imposing but rather familiar and welcoming.

'Sorry. I wanted you to sleep for as long as possible.' Slowly he came into the room and she watched him move, her body breaking out into a mass of tingles as he came and sat beside her.

She sighed and knew she'd never get tired of seeing him, of being with him, and as he tenderly pushed her hair back from her face Aracely acknowledged the truth of her feelings. Sick she might be, stuffy head she might have, but the message from her heart was crystal clear. She'd fallen in love with Trent Mornington.

'Feeling better?'

'Yes.'

'Good.'

'Thank you,' she said.

'For?'

'Everything. Being here. Looking after Robby.'

'My pleasure.' He caressed her cheek.

'How did clinic go?'

'Non-eventful. Everyone was concerned for you but pleased you were being looked after.'

'Good.' Then she gasped. 'Oh. House calls.'

'I've contacted the district nurse and she said she can cover you for today and tomorrow.'

'But Uncle Robert—'

'She said if she had any trouble with him, she'd call.'

Aracely relaxed a little, taking a sip from the

glass of water by her bed. 'And Maggie? I hope I haven't given her this cold. It'll be the last thing she needs.'

'She's fine. Everyone's fine. Just stop worrying for a moment and concentrate on getting better,' he ordered, leaning closer.

'No.' She put a hand between them. 'Don't kiss me. I don't want you to get this either.'

Trent took her hand from his chest and continued to close the distance between them, pressing his lips to hers. 'Too late for that,' he said softly, and the way he looked at her made her wonder if he was only referring to the cold. She couldn't move, didn't want to, and kissed him back with all the new found love in her heart.

'Trent?' came Robby's voice and they broke apart, both smiling. 'The microwave's stopped. Now what do I do?'

'Microwave?' she asked. 'What's he doing with the microwave?'

'He's fine. Back in a moment.' Trent disappeared and Aracely raised a hand to her lips, still feeling the warmth of where his mouth had just been. She loved him. She wasn't sure how or when it had happened but it had, and with that realisation came a whole heap of questions and problems. What would happen next? Trent had a life in Sydney, despite what he'd said on the subject, and would be returning there at the end of the week.

Robby carefully carried in a tray of food and Aracely immediately sat up, taking it from him with thanks. When Robby allowed himself to be picked up by Trent, winding his arms around Trent's neck, Aracely realised her son was as much attached to the man as she was. What had she done? Opened not only herself up to the possible hurt but she might also have endangered her son's emotions.

'It's chicken soup. Aunty Maggie made it and Trent said it will make you better. Will it make you better, Mummy?'

Aracely took a sip and nodded. 'Soup and lots of cuddles and kisses,' she told him, although this time she couldn't help but encompass Trent in those words. He raised his eyebrows suggestively, as though he was more than willing to help in that area as well.

He'd asked her last night if they could try dating and she'd agreed, so for now the fact that he would be leaving soon needed to be pushed aside and she'd simply have to deal with whatever happened next week when it came. She'd survived emotional upheaval before, she could do it again. Couldn't she?

On Tuesday and Wednesday, Aracely felt much better and by Thursday she was back to her usual self. After dropping Robby at preschool, both she and Trent headed around to see Uncle Robert.

Aracely knocked on the door. 'Uncle Robert?' she called when she received no answer. 'It's me. Aracely.' She knocked again, her anxiety increasing the longer it took for him to respond. She'd had a report from the district nurse that although Uncle Robert's blood pressure had been quite high, he'd assured her he'd been taking the tablets. Aracely *wanted* to believe him but also knew how he could pull the wool over other people's eyes, other people who didn't know him as well as she did.

'Uncle Robert,' she called and knocked again. 'It's me.'

In the next instant she heard the lock click and then the door was flung wide open. 'I know who you are, girlie. My memory's not going,' he grumbled.

'Then why didn't you answer the door the first time I knocked?' When she stepped in, she thought he looked more tired than usual and instinctively knew he hadn't taken any medication since the last pill she'd forced down him.

'Thought it was that pesky district nurse.'

'Uncle Robert,' she scolded lightly as she followed him to the kitchen, his favourite room. 'The woman's just trying to do her job and, besides, if you hadn't answered the door, she would have got the staff from the retirement office and they'd have broken in here, no doubt concerned and panicked for your health and well-being, only to find you sitting at the table, enjoying a drink.' She picked up the bottle. 'You're not supposed to be drinking beer.' She took it to the sink, emptying the contents down the drain.

'I was drinking that,' he grumbled, then sighed. 'Man can't even enjoy a beer in his own home.'

He looked forlorn as she tossed the bottle into the recycle bin. 'Bossy little thing. Just like my sister.'

'Don't you forget it.'

'Trent. You'll need to do something about that,' Uncle Robert said in a conspiratorial whisper. 'Hey, where's my little mate?'

'At preschool. You know that.'

Uncle Robert nodded sadly. 'Just wanted to see him but it's probably just as well.'

Aracely paused in the act of taking her sphygmomanometer from her backpack. 'Why? What's wrong? I know you haven't been taking your tablets. I can tell.'

'Oh, calm down now, girlie. I don't have much time. So, Trent. What do you think of Port Wallaby?'

Trent sized up the man in front of him and knew honesty was definitely the order of the day. No platitudes for Uncle Robert, simply the honest-to-goodness truth. 'I'm falling in love with it the more I see of it.'

'Is that so?' Uncle Robert leaned back in his chair. 'And would you say the same about my niece?'

'Uncle Robert!' Aracely was appalled. 'That really is—'

'Oh, hold your tongue. I'm not asking you. I'm asking him.' He stabbed an arthritic finger at Trent. 'Well, boy. What say you?'

Trent held the old man's stare for a moment longer before turning to look at Aracely. His eyes softened as he took in her total embarrassment and he couldn't help the smile that touched his lips.

His eyes were a caress as they swept over her and she felt as though he'd touched every deep part of her, every facet of her being. Her breath caught in her throat and tingles exploded as she waited for him to answer. Did he?

Trent opened his mouth to speak but Uncle Robert cut him off before he could begin.

'That's what I thought. Now I can rest,' he said softly, then promptly slumped across the kitchen table.

Aracely was frozen for a split second but in the next instant Trent had his fingers pressed to the old man's carotid pulse and she was by her uncle's side, shaking him gently.

'Uncle Robert. Uncle Robert!'

'Pulse is there but weak,' Trent reported, holding out his hand for the sphygmo. She quickly passed it over before searching in her backpack for the stethoscope, eager to listen to Uncle Robert's heart.

'Heartbeat is faint.'

'What meds has he been on?'

'Nifedipine.'

'I don't suppose you have some?'

Again, Aracely rummaged through the backpack with anxiety and eagerness. 'Only in tablet form.'

'Break it up before we get him to swallow it. That way it'll be fast-acting.'

Uncle Robert started moaning and Aracely called to him, checking his pupils with her medical torch. 'What?' he mumbled, and she realised he was very hot.

'Why do you do this?' she accused lovingly, before crossing to the sink to get a glass of water. She returned to his side, making him swallow the crushed tablets.

'Have you been sick?' Trent asked, after telling Aracely that his blood pressure reading was extremely high.

'Earlier,' was all he said, totally out of breath. 'Help me shift him to the floor.'

'Wait.' Aracely raced up the hallway and pulled a large blanket from the linen cupboard, returning quickly to lay it open on the floor. 'This will make it easier when we need to move him and also more comfortable.' She bent and kissed her uncle's head.

'Let me go, girl,' he whispered, and tears instantly filled her eyes. She blinked them away.

'It's not check-out time just yet, mate,' she replied softly, as they moved him to lie down. Aracely snapped her phone off her waistband and called through to Moonta hospital, letting them know the situation.

'Will they send an ambulance?' Trent asked.

'We can get him there faster,' she said. The sooner we can get him onto an IV drip, the better. Besides, the sister at Moonta said the ambulance is currently on its way back from Kadina, which means it would take them about thirty minutes to get here.'

'No…fuss,' Uncle Robert muttered.

'Fuss?' she said with mock disbelief. 'As if

we'd make a fuss for you. No. No fussing,' she promised, taking a breath and calming down. 'Helping—yes. Fussing—no.'

'You're fussing,' Trent said, and Aracely almost cried with relief when she saw a smile touch Uncle Robert's mouth.

'He's good for you, girlie. Keep him.'

'Shush now and let me fuss,' she returned. Trent took Uncle Robert's blood pressure again.

'Mild improvement but not much. We'd best be moving.'

Aracely nodded and raced around the small two bedroom unit, grabbing a bag and putting pyjamas, toothbrush, comb and shaver in, as well as quickly packing some clothes and a few of his favourite books.

Trent had packed up the backpack, leaving the sphygmo, stethoscope and medical torch out so he could continue to monitor Uncle Robert. They managed to transfer him to the back of her four-wheel-drive after lowering the seats down to make more room, propping his legs up with some cushions Aracely had collected.

'You stay in the back and monitor him,' she said as she climbed behind the wheel and started the engine. They didn't talk much on the drive, Aracely concentrating on the road and also navigating the now crossable creek.

When they arrived at Moonta hospital, the clinical nurse consultant, Jill Ozeransky, had a barouche waiting for them and came out with one of the porters.

'I need him hooked up to an IV with sodium nitroprusside. Monitor via ECG for cardiac dysrhythmias. Patient has vomited and lost consciousness but only for a few minutes. He's had one nifedipine tablet and BP was initially 210 over 120 but is now down to 200 over 110.' Aracely spoke as they transferred Uncle Robert to the barouche and wheeled him in out of the cold into the nice warm hospital.

'Right you are,' Jill replied as they took Uncle Robert's barouche into the treatment room, getting an IV organised and hooking him up to the ECG machine to monitor his heart. He was started on IV fluids as well as monitoring his blood pressure and oxygen levels.

Aracely stood back and looked at her uncle, the man who was almost one hundred years old, and seeing him lying there, so small and pale with tubes and wires coming out of him left, right and centre, she couldn't help the tears that gathered in her eyes.

'I'm going to call Maggie,' she said, needing some space. She rushed out of the hospital's front door and stood for a moment, looking up the big gum trees across the road, trying to breathe around the pain in her heart.

'Aracely?' She turned quickly to see Trent come out.

'Is something wrong?' she asked with in-creased concern.

'No. No change. I've ordered a few tests. I hope you don't mind.'

'No.' She shook her head and looked back at the trees. 'How am I going to tell Mags?'

Trent placed his hand around her shoulder and she leant against him without hesitation, loving the fact that she had someone supportive at this time. 'You tell her Uncle Robert's not well and to meet you here.' He pulled the phone from her waistband and held it out to her. 'You can do this.'

'He just looked so…old.'

'He *is* old, Cely, and maybe he's right? Maybe it's time to face up to the fact that at some point you'll have to let him go.'

'I can't. I just can't, Trent. He means the world to me, he always has.' Tears streamed down her face as she spoke before she turned her face into his chest and sobbed.

She was already letting go. He could hear it in the way she cried, feel it in her body, see it in her eyes. As he held her, he realised with a flash of clarity that he didn't want to leave her. He wanted to stay, to help her through the next few weeks at least, but more to the point he wanted to be there to help her through everything because he realised he was in love with her.

When her crying started to settle, he offered her a handkerchief before holding her phone out to her once more. 'Call Maggie. Get Billy to bring her and also see if they can pick up Robby.'

'Robby?'

'He needs to see Uncle Robert, too.'

'No. He'll get upset. *I'm* upset, seeing him all hooked up to wires and machines, and I'm a grown woman *and* a doctor!'

'Robby's a smart kid, Aracely. It will help him understand what's happened to Uncle Robert and, as much as you'd like to, you can't protect him from the pain he's going to feel. He needs the chance to say goodbye just as much as you and Maggie do.'

'I don't want to say goodbye.' Her lower lip wobbled again.

'I know,' he soothed, and pressed the phone into her hand. 'Lean on me, Cely. Let me be strong for you.'

Aracely looked deeply into his eyes, her love for him pouring into her heart. He was here and he was offering to help her yet again. She called her sister, letting her know the situation. When she'd finished, she looked up at Trent.

'You're quite a man,' she whispered, and pressed her mouth to his in a kiss of thanks.

He didn't try to pull her to him, though he wanted to. He didn't try to devour her mouth, though he wanted that more than anything at the moment. Instead, he simply brushed his hand tenderly across her cheek and looked down into her eyes. 'You're welcome, Cely. *Very* welcome.'

She was unable to speak for a moment, the intensity, the reality of just how powerful her feelings were for this man hitting home with force. They went back inside and stood on either side of the bed.

Uncle Robert roused after a few minutes and looked at her.

'Cely?'

'I'm here,' she said quickly, and took his hand in hers. 'See? I'm here.'

'It's time to let me go, girlie.'

'I don't know if I can.' Tears slid silently down her cheeks.

'Trent?'

'Yes, sir?'

Uncle Robert rasped out a laugh that sounded more like a cough while he groped for Trent's hand. 'I ain't no sir, I keep telling you.' He brought both Trent's and Aracely's hands together above him. 'You take care of my Cely,' he said firmly.

'Yes.'

'She and her boy need you.'

Trent nodded and lifted his eyes to meet Aracely's. 'I need them, too.'

Uncle Robert dropped his hands back to his sides and sighed heavily, as though a huge weight had just been lifted from his shoulders. Aracely stood there, holding Trent's hand, unable to believe what had just happened.

One of the machines started beeping and they dropped their linked hands, springing into action, trying to stabilise him. 'The drip was too fast,' Trent commented. 'I've slowed it down. He should stabilise now.'

'What does that mean?' Maggie asked from the entry to the cubicle. Billy was behind her with Robby in his arms. The boy instantly went to Aracely.

'We don't want to lower the blood pressure too much. Hypertension can easily turn into hypotension, which is low blood pressure,' Trent explained.

'And if it dropped too fast?'

'He could have a stroke or a heart attack and that's just the icing on the cake,' Trent continued.

'Is Uncle Robert going to die?' Robby asked, and Aracely found it impossible to work any words past the lump of pain in her throat.

'Yes, mate,' Trent answered, and came around the bed to put his arm about Aracely's shoulders.

'Oh. When he dies, can I still play with him?' Robby's eyes were wide and innocent and at his words Aracely gasped in pain and she felt Trent's hand tighten on her shoulder.

'No, mate.' It was Trent who once more delivered the bad news. 'It's time to say goodbye to Uncle Robert.'

The old man slipped into a coma during the night. Robby and Maggie were in a spare hospital room, sleeping. Billy and Trent were talking quietly in the corner and Aracely was holding her uncle's hand, watching him slip away from her.

'His body's been through severe trauma and for a man his age that's tough to come through,' Trent said softly, crossing to her side and pulling her into his arms.

'His organs are starting to shut down.' Aracely turned her face into Trent's chest, letting him hold her. She had no energy to think about how close they'd become in the last few days. She only knew that she needed him and he was there for her. He was so different from Jaden, that much was clear, and she could only hope that what he'd said to Uncle Robert was the truth and not just a line to placate a dying man.

When it was time, she woke Maggie and picked Robby up, all of them crowding around Uncle Robert's bed. They all said goodbye and hugged each other. Just before dawn on Friday morning, the ninety-four-year-old man passed away.

Aracely knew Uncle Robert had gone to a better place, that he was now free from pain, and although she wanted him there to talk to him, to laugh with him, to listen to him, she knew it was for the best.

Time passed in a blur of phone calls, paperwork and arrangements. As the day wore on, Trent watched Aracely become more exhausted, Robby beginning to try his mother's very thin patience.

'Take them home,' Maggie said, handing him a set of car keys. 'Take our car. I can drive Aracely's with all its modifications.'

'Thanks, Mags.' Trent nodded. 'You take care, now.'

'I will. You just worry about my sister, OK?'

'Deal.'

Maggie stood and kissed his cheek. 'I'm glad you came pounding on her door last week, Trent. You're good for her.' She left before he could reply. He managed to convince Aracely to come home and after he'd fed Robby a bowl of porridge for dinner—which the four-year-old found very amusing—and settled him to sleep, he went to find Aracely staring out the window into the dark night.

He crossed to her side and slipped his arms about her. 'How are you doing?'

'I feel numb.'

'That's understandable.' Neither of them moved for quite some time but eventually Aracely shifted in his arms to face him.

'Do you need to go tomorrow?'

'Yes.'

'I don't want you to.'

'I don't want to either but it's the responsible thing to do. I have patients, clinics, operating lists.'

'I know.' She broke away from him. 'I know. It's responsible and it's what you need to do, and you have people waiting for you, depending on you, but I don't have to like it.' Aracely wound her loose hair on top of her head and secured it in a knot. 'I feel so alone.'

'But I'm here.'

'Not for long. You're leaving me. Uncle Robert's left me.' She shook her head. 'It's all happening again. Jaden left me.'

'I thought you left him?'

Aracely shook her head. 'Physically I was the one to do the leaving but mentally Jaden left me long before that.'

'What happened, Cely? Talk to me. Share with me.' He held out his hand and she took it, turning it over in hers before speaking softly.

'Jaden was a man with direction. When we met he was so…driven. He had purpose, he knew exactly what he wanted and nothing was going to get in his way. I liked that. I was drawn to that.'

'It doesn't sound like you.'

'Well, not now but back then…back then I had just started my surgical rotation and I was loving it. I knew that surgery was hard, meant long hours, meant you had next to no private life. I was prepared for that and was ready to give it everything I had. Jaden inspired me. He had charisma and charm and knew the right thing to say and I was…caught. We used to sit at the same table in the cafeteria and whenever our schedules meshed we'd eat together—that's how we met.' She sighed sadly. 'Now it seems as though it happened to someone else.'

'I know how that feels.'

'Yes. Yes, you do, don't you?' Her words were eager and she was positive he understood her completely. She raised his hand to her lips and kissed it, loving the way his skin felt against her mouth.

'So what happened?' he prompted, not only to get her to continue but also in an attempt to try and control the urge to haul her close.

'We got married and it was great…for the first few months. Jaden had big dreams as well as a head for business and administration. Medical Director for the entire hospital. That was his goal and nothing was getting in his way. In those first few months we attended so many fundraisers and functions and shook hands with politicians and listened politely to people make speeches, all so we could take their money for the hospital.'

'How did that fit in with your schedule?'

'Not too well sometimes, but Jaden would often arrange for my shifts to be changed so I could attend as his pretty wife who was training to be a surgeon. You see, I realised all too late that his real motivation for marrying me was purely political. He didn't love me. He wanted to be surrounded by success. Having a wife who was a successful surgeon meant *he* was successful in his private life.'

'Medical directors rarely do surgery, let alone a lot of medicine.'

'Exactly. If he was married to a surgeon, then it would show that he still had his finger on the pulse...although I doubt he would have listened to a word I had to say on *any* topic. The last I heard, he'd remarried and was working in Hobart. Have you heard of the new Women's and Children's hospital in Hobart?'

'Yes.'

'That's Jaden. He had a vision and he followed

through, providing a much-needed resource. It means that patients no longer need to be flown to the children's hospital in Melbourne when they're critical.'

'He's doing good work.' Trent nodded.

'Yes. He's doing what he'd planned to do. I just didn't fit into that plan.'

'And Robby? How did he factor into Jaden's carefully laid plans?'

Aracely dipped her head and shook it sadly. 'He didn't. Jaden was furious and even accused me of having an affair.' She laughed without humour. 'As if I had the time.'

'He didn't want a child?'

'Ironic, really, considering the work he does now, but he told me it would mess things up.' She looked at him, their gazes holding as she spoke the words clearly and concisely. 'He wanted me to have an abortion.'

'What?'

'A child didn't fit in with the plan. Wasn't factored into the plan. Had never even been mentioned, discussed or scheduled.'

Trent clenched his jaw, grinding his teeth

together in repressed fury and frustration. He couldn't believe that a man would just leave someone like Aracely. She was amazing and beautiful and intelligent and the need to protect her— not only her but her son as well—protect them from all further hurts was overpowering. He shook his head, knowing he could never leave a child of his, especially one as terrific as Robby. He forced himself to calm down and looked at the woman beside him. 'And then you had your accident.'

'And my world changed once more. For a while there I thought we might have been given a second chance. He was there, by my side— stunned I hadn't lost the baby—but by my side. Then the more my pregnancy started to show, the more he withdrew. Finally, two months before Robby's birth, I knew for certain the marriage was over, and headed home here where I had all the love and support I needed.'

'You've done a brilliant job. Robby is… Cely, he's amazing.'

She smiled easily. 'Yes, he is. He's too young to understand what happened and old enough to accept that he's doing all right without a dad.'

The smile started to slip. 'I know that'll change.' She paused and sighed optimistically. 'But he has Billy and my father and Uncle…' She stopped and dragged in a breath, feeling Trent's grip tighten on her hand. 'Anyway, it's not as though he doesn't have any male role models.'

He murmured his agreement. 'Good ol' Uncle Billy, who hurtles headlong into danger.'

'Yep. That's our Billy and we love him. So Robby and I continue with our life here. We're happy. We're comfortable and content.'

'Really?'

'Yes…or at least we were…until you showed up.' Aracely shifted and raised her hand to touch his cheek.

'When I came pounding on your door?'

'Scaring me half to death.'

'I'm sorry.'

'You're forgiven.' She leaned forward and pressed a small kiss to his lips. 'You said that we should try and date this week and I have to tell you that with everything that's happened, with me being sick and with Uncle Robert…' She paused and took a deep breath. 'Trent, I want to

LUCY CLARK 273

do more than just date you. My life has shown me, and today has only rammed that message home, that I just can't wait for things to happen, that when I feel something...when someone is special to me, I need to take action. Life is far too short, Trent.' She met his gaze and held it. 'I've fallen in love with you.'

His jaw dropped open and his eyes widened. Aracely continued in a rush.

'I don't expect that to make any difference to you leaving because I know that has to happen and I don't want you to feel as though I'm trying to trap you or put a noose around you or anything like that. I...' She shrugged. 'I just wanted you to know. You have a right to know.'

'Aracely,' he began, but she held up her hand to stop him.

'Please. You don't need to say anything or rationalise or anything like that. I just needed to tell you.' With that, she turned and headed to her room.

Trent didn't sleep much that night and as a consequence was up bright and early the next morning. It appeared the same could be said for

Aracely as he found her in the kitchen, drinking her second cup of coffee.

'Hi,' she said, feeling a little self-conscious, and quickly offered him a cup. He took it from her and then bent to kiss her.

'Good morning, Cely.' Robby came into the kitchen, still in his pyjamas but wide awake, Mr Rabbit in tow. 'And good morning to you, too, Robby.' Trent put his cup on the bench then gathered the boy into his arms, tickling his tummy. 'As we're all up and awake, how about a walk along the beach?'

'What time does your flight leave?' Aracely asked.

'Not until this afternoon. So we have plenty of time to collect shells and stones and just spend time together.'

'Yay.' Robby wiggled free of Trent's arms and rushed to his room.

'Get dressed,' Aracely called after him. 'And put your gumboots on, not your runners.'

'OK, Mummy,' came the reply.

Aracely looked to Trent. 'You're in a good mood today.'

'That's because it's the first day of the rest of my life,' he said, and after pressing another kiss to her lips picked up his coffee-cup and walked out of the kitchen, leaving her confused and wondering.

There was nothing left for her to do but to get ready and to make sure her son was bundled up for a walk on the beach on a fresh winter's morning. Trent took her left hand as they headed down to Gates beach.

'It seems so long ago.' Trent scanned the calm ocean as they headed out to the rock pools, Robby picking up little rocks and shells and putting them into his bucket. They could walk easily on the spider web-like rock yet the area had been so dangerous that stormy night they'd met. There was no sign of the boat wreckage, which had either been cleaned up or washed out to sea.

'Hey, Robby,' Trent called. 'Look at that.' He pointed to a hermit crab scuttling around, and they all watched. It was as though they were a family, out having a morning at the beach, and Aracely's heart wanted so much for it to be real.

When they came to the big rock standing large

and firm in the middle of the rock pools, Trent paused. He raised his free hand and ran it slowly down the rock's surface, mesmerised by the tactile sensation.

'We were anchored to this rock,' he said. 'It saved us. Saved us all. If it hadn't been here, we wouldn't have been able to reach the boat.'

'It's a wonder you all survived.'

'Agreed.'

She turned to face him. 'Trent, not many people walk away from such danger as you did.'

'I know.' He paused, staring out into the blue ocean. 'It changes things.' His grip tightened on her hand and, after calling to Robby, they made their way back to the beach in silence.

'You like being here, don't you?' he asked.

'Of course. It's my home.'

'No plans to do surgery?'

'No. I can't. You know that.'

'I know you could do anything you put your mind to, Aracely. We've discussed this before and while I can see you're happy here being a GP, I don't want you to feel as though that's all you can do.'

'I have an injured hand,' she reiterated. Trent merely raised her left hand to his lips and kissed it.

'Why should that stop you? You've modified your car.' He shrugged. 'What's to stop you from modifying a surgery so you could operate?'

She thought about that for a moment. 'Nothing.'

'There you go, then. Should you decide to pursue your dream of surgery in the future, there's nothing stopping you. It won't be easy but, then, neither is running a successful GP practice and raising a child on your own, yet you're excelling at both of those things.'

'The thing is, I'm not sure if… What I mean is… I'm really happy doing what I'm doing. Besides, my job gives me the flexibility I need with Robby.'

'You also happen to be an extremely good GP,' he offered. 'You're an amazing woman, Aracely.' He stopped walking and turned her to face him. 'Last night you told me you love me—'

'Trent…I…'

'You left without giving me the opportunity to tell you how I feel.'

'But you don't need to. I didn't say it to pull confessions from you.'

He smiled at that. 'No. You're not that sort of woman, Aracely, and that's one of the things I love most about you. You accept people for who they are, for what they can give, and then you simply love them.'

She blinked in the early morning light. 'You…?' She trailed off, unsure she'd heard him correctly.

'Love you? Yes. I do. Very much.'

'But you're leaving today.'

'True, but it won't be for long. I mentioned before that although I work in Sydney, it's not where I live. Until I met you, I had no idea where that was.' He checked where Robby was. It was pure instinct now that made him aware of the child's movements, to make sure he was safe at all times. 'You and Robby feel so…right. It's as though I've been living in the dark for the past five years and now I've finally found the light. You, Cely. You and Robby are my light. Do you have any idea what it's like to live in constant darkness?'

'Yes,' she answered quickly. 'I know exactly what it's like. Robby was my light, Trent. He gave me hope, he renewed me, but until you burst into our lives last week I didn't realise the light wasn't as bright or as brilliant as it could be. So, yes, I know exactly where you're coming from.' She giggled. 'I can't believe how happy I am. How gloriously happy I am.' She sighed. 'It's because of you.'

'I want to move here, Cely. I'll return to Sydney this afternoon and start the ball rolling because I know for a fact that I won't be able to stay away from you and Robby for long. You—both of you—are the family I've been yearning for, the family I feel as though I lost.'

Aracely touched his cheek lovingly. 'We *are* your family. Know that for a fact, but what about the rest of your family? Your parents? Your siblings?' She paused. 'Your cousin?'

'They are who they are,' he said slowly, as though he was carefully choosing his words. 'I can't change them but you have taught me to accept them. For who they are, for what they can give, and to be satisfied with that. If they don't live up to my expectations, well, perhaps I need to lower my expectations. Last week, after spending time with you, I began to realise that the wall I'd built around myself for protection

wasn't necessary any more. I didn't need protection any more because I had you. It took me a
while to figure it out but I got there in the end.'

'I'm happy for you.'

'Happy for us, I think.'

She smiled. 'Most definitely.' Trent kissed her,
then called Robby over.

'How many shells and rocks have you got in
your bucket there?' he asked, and Robby shook
the bucket, the stones and shells, making a heavy
noise. 'Sounds like enough.'

'What for? Are we gonna play a game?' Robby
asked, sitting down and instantly tipping them over.

'Sort of. I thought we might do some spelling.
We'll make some letters and see if Mummy can
guess what they spell.'

'I can write my name,' Robby said, as Trent
crouched down and started to arrange the stones
and shells. Robby wrote his name in the sand and
both Aracely and Trent praised him for his effort.

'Can you spell the word "me"?' Trent asked.

'Yep.'

'OK. You make the word "me" over here. Spell
it out with the stones and shells.'

'Can I help?' Aracely asked.

'You have to close your eyes, Mummy,' Robby declared, so Aracely, even though she was bursting with excitement and happiness, knowing exactly what Trent was doing, closed her eyes and waited. She didn't have to wait long and when she was finally allowed to open them, she couldn't help but laugh, her answer to the question posed reflected in her eyes.

Trent and Robby stood in front of her, their handiwork on display at their feet, both males grinning brightly. Robby, bless his heart, had indeed written the word 'me' but as he was still learning to write, he'd made a 'w' instead of an 'm', so what Aracely saw written in the sand with brightly coloured shells and stones were the words MARRY WE. She thought it was absolutely perfect.

EPILOGUE

ARACELY started down the path to the beach, her heart filled with nervous happiness. Her father was by her side, holding tight to her arm, and Maggie, resplendent in a gown the colour of the setting sun, went before her as her matron of honour. She only wished that Uncle Robert could have been there to share their special day, but knew in her heart that her beloved uncle would be smiling down on them.

She could see Trent waiting impatiently on the beach, Robby and Billy beside him. Her mother was holding Maggie's two-week-old baby girl, pleased to have had her first granddaughter delivered safe and sound.

Trent's parents and a few of his siblings were among the crowd gathered informally on Gates beach for the sunset wedding. Dan, Phil and

Greg—Trent's closest friends from medical school—had also made the trek back to the beach for the wedding, and she was glad to see them all looking much healthier than the last time they'd been there.

Aracely breathed a sigh of relief, unable to believe this day had finally arrived. She'd waited a long time for her happily ever after and today it had arrived.

After Trent had resigned from the hospital and moved to Port Wallaby, he'd had no problem gaining employment with Peninsula Medical Services, who were more than willing to snap up a permanent orthopaedic surgeon for the area.

When she eventually reached his side, she only had eyes for him and he for her. The wedding celebrant said a few words and then it was time for Trent and Aracely to say the vows they'd written.

'Trent. You burst into my life—literally—and here on this beach we saved lives. Not only those of your friends but each other's. You are the light of my life and, along with Robby, I can't wait for the three of us to become a family. My love for you is so strong, I know we can weather any storm and embrace all the blessings coming our way. I take you as my husband today in front of our friends and family. I ask that they be witnesses to our love—a love that will last for ever.'

'Aracely. You have provided me with a haven, a place where I can be myself and be accepted as I am. You have shown me the way home and now that I'm here, now that I've found you and Robby, I won't ever let you go. I love you with all my heart. I promise to be an amazing husband and father, knowing we will work things out together. Without you, I am an empty shell. Fill me with your happiness, your love and your laughter. Be with me for ever, my darling Cely.'

Robby stepped between them, holding out the rings. Both Aracely and Trent knelt down. Trent helped Robby place the ring on Aracely's finger.

'I love you, Mummy,' the boy said.

Then he turned and with Aracely's help, they put the ring on Trent's finger together.

'I love you, my new daddy.'

There wasn't a dry eye on the beach as the sun slid down behind the horizon, the sky bathed in glorious shades of oranges, pinks and reds.

'Red sky at night, shepherd's delight,' she whispered softly, after the celebrant had pronounced them husband and wife.

'Who cares about the shepherd?' Trent returned, pulling her close for another kiss. 'You're my delight.'

Aracely laughed, happier than she'd ever thought she had a right to be, and knew their shared delight would last them a lifetime.

MEDICAL™

Large Print

Titles for the next six months…

January

SINGLE DAD, OUTBACK WIFE	Amy Andrews
A WEDDING IN THE VILLAGE	Abigail Gordon
IN HIS ANGEL'S ARMS	Lynne Marshall
THE FRENCH DOCTOR'S MIDWIFE BRIDE	Fiona Lowe
A FATHER FOR HER SON	Rebecca Lang
THE SURGEON'S MARRIAGE PROPOSAL	Molly Evans

February

THE ITALIAN GP'S BRIDE	Kate Hardy
THE CONSULTANT'S ITALIAN KNIGHT	Maggie Kingsley
HER MAN OF HONOUR	Melanie Milburne
ONE SPECIAL NIGHT…	Margaret McDonagh
THE DOCTOR'S PREGNANCY SECRET	Leah Martyn
BRIDE FOR A SINGLE DAD	Laura Iding

March

THE SINGLE DAD'S MARRIAGE WISH	Carol Marinelli
THE PLAYBOY DOCTOR'S PROPOSAL	Alison Roberts
THE CONSULTANT'S SURPRISE CHILD	Joanna Neil
DR FERRERO'S BABY SECRET	Jennifer Taylor
THEIR VERY SPECIAL CHILD	Dianne Drake
THE SURGEON'S RUNAWAY BRIDE	Olivia Gates

 MILLS & BOON®

Pure reading pleasure

1207 LP 2P P1 Medical

MEDICAL™

Large Print

April

THE ITALIAN COUNT'S BABY   Amy Andrews
THE NURSE HE'S BEEN WAITING FOR   Meredith Webber
HIS LONG-AWAITED BRIDE   Jessica Matthews
A WOMAN TO BELONG TO   Fiona Lowe
WEDDING AT PELICAN BEACH   Emily Forbes
DR CAMPBELL'S SECRET SON   Anne Fraser

May

THE MAGIC OF CHRISTMAS   Sarah Morgan
THEIR LOST-AND-FOUND FAMILY   Marion Lennox
CHRISTMAS BRIDE-TO-BE   Alison Roberts
HIS CHRISTMAS PROPOSAL   Lucy Clark
BABY: FOUND AT CHRISTMAS   Laura Iding
THE DOCTOR'S PREGNANCY BOMBSHELL   Janice Lynn

June

CHRISTMAS EVE BABY   Caroline Anderson
LONG-LOST SON: BRAND-NEW FAMILY   Lilian Darcy
THEIR LITTLE CHRISTMAS MIRACLE   Jennifer Taylor
TWINS FOR A CHRISTMAS BRIDE   Josie Metcalfe
THE DOCTOR'S VERY SPECIAL   Kate Hardy
CHRISTMAS
A PREGNANT NURSE'S CHRISTMAS   Meredith Webber
WISH

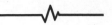 MILLS & BOON®
Pure reading pleasure

1207 LP 2P P2 Medical